THE GLASS PEDESTAL

The Glass Pedestal

By

Cheyenne Maryland Quinn

Terra Quinn Press

The Glass Pedestal

First Edition: July 2026

ISBN: 979-8-234-12260-5

Published by Terra Quinn Press

Cover design by Siiri Becker (Ultrasonic)

Printed in the United States of America

Prologue: The View from the Horizon

In the early months of her thirties, Sasha had the world completely ahead of her, even if she couldn't always see the horizon.

She was, by any definition, a stunning catch. Standing five-foot-six with sun-tanned skin and long, flowing, bleached-blond hair, she possessed a naturally fit, toned physique that drew eyes the moment she entered a room. She was a blond bombshell with a brilliant mind to match, though she carried her beauty with a quiet, unassuming modesty. She didn't fully know her own worth; she didn't realize the gravity she pulled.

Her twenties had been a masterclass in settling for less than she deserved. There had been a failed marriage to a deadbeat husband who took far more than he ever contributed, followed by a complicated, draining affair with a co-worker that left her emotionally exhausted. She had spent years pouring her energy into men who treated her worth as disposable, leaving her own desires on the back burner.

But as a New York winter began to settle in, a quiet shift occurred inside her. The past was in the rearview mirror. The dust from the old heartbreaks had finally settled, and the slate was clean.

She was fit, she was sharp, and she was ready. It was finally time for her to have the man she actually deserved—someone who would match her energy, admire her intellect, and value her loyalty. She wanted a real partnership, a beautiful romance, a clean start.

She didn't know that the demon was already waiting for her, sitting in the dim light of a local tavern, nursing a vodka handle and looking for his next masterpiece.

CHAPTER 1: *The Siren Song of Arrogance*

It was a smoldering hot and sunny day in May, and Sasha just walked into the bar on the main strip downtown to meet her ex-flame, now platonic friend, Jerry, for some drinks. As she walked in, the bar was packed, packed with men. This didn't bother her; she just pushed her way through them towards the bar to order a drink. She was standing tightly behind this one guy who was ordering a Labatt Blue bottle. He turned around and almost ran into her; their eyes met, they laughed, and he moved to give her space at the bar, gesturing for her to belly up to the bar with his hand. Sasha squeezed up to the bar to order.

"Jack and Coke, please," Sasha told the bartender confidently, with a smile; she always smiled.

"Hi there," the Labatt Blue guy said to her.

"Hi, thanks, I thought I was never going to get to order," Sasha replied. Sasha's breath was taken away. *This guy is so sexy, he even smells sexy*. She thought, totally enthralled.

Jerry wanders in, and they grab a bar table as the bar is too busy to sit at; they chat about their lives. Sasha knows there is nothing between them anymore, at least not in her mind; she knows that he was just a rebound to get away from her drab husband and not be sexually deprived while making her exit.

"Looks like the bar is clearing out, you want to go sit there, I need a drink anyway?" Sasha asked Jerry.

"Yeah, let's sit there, I need a shot, it's been a long day," Jerry replied. The two moved up to the open bar stools. The guy who literally almost bumped into Sasha was sitting in the seat next to the two open seats. *How convenient,* Sasha thought to herself, almost creaming her pants as she sat down.

"Jerry, what brings you here on this Friday?" The sexy mystery man blurted to Jerry. *Oh my, they know each other*. Sasha wasn't sure if she should be worried or if she should be content with this acquaintance.

“Meeting my friend Sasha for a few, we used to...well, she and I used to work together,” Jerry said, hesitating to go into any more detail. “Jeff, this is Sasha, Sasha, this is Jeff.” Jerry introduced the two. “Jeff works for his brother's HVAC business in town, that’s how we know each other; we go way back,” Jerry said. Sasha barely heard a word Jerry said, she could not take her eyes off of Jeff, His blue eyes, his tanned skin, his flowing brown hair peeking out from under a dirty baseball cap. As Sasha listened to the two guys chat, she could hear the arrogance in Jeff’s voice; he was confident, too confident, but there was something about him she liked.

They indulged in a few drinks together while the guys talked shop, then Jeff whispered something in Jerry’s ear, and Jerry’s mood shifted instantly. It was time to leave. Jerry was uncomfortable, and he wasn’t leaving Sasha there either; they had to go together, even though they had driven separately and sure weren’t going home together.

"Hey, it's getting late, we'd better get going," Jerry said to Sasha. He clearly didn't want to leave Sasha alone with this handsome, yet mysterious man. *What did this Jeff guy say to Jerry to make him want to bust out of here so abruptly?* Sasha wondered.

"I suppose it has been a long week," She replied to Jerry. "Hey, very nice meeting you, Jeff," Sasha said to Jeff as she got up from her barstool and began walking out.

"My pleasure," Jeff replied.

Sasha got home. *Oh my god, I cannot get that face out of my head, he is so sexy, what a handsome devil,* she thought, with the sensation of butterflies in her gut. He was maybe five foot seven or so, with that brightly tanned skin and a dirty Buffalo Sabers hat that suggested a long day of hard work, *an honorable man with an honest profession*, she thought. There was something about his posture, the way he held his drink cocked against his chest, and that rugged, bow-legged stance that played on a loop in her mind. He was confident, and she admired that. Still curious what had upset Jerry enough to just leave the bar, what could this Jeff guy have possibly said to Jerry? *Oh well, that's Jerry's problem*, not paying it any mind any longer. Sasha went about her evening routine: a bath, a hair masque, a face masque, a tan in her hallway tanning bed by her bedroom, and TV in bed.

By midnight, she was still awake in her king-sized bed, *this bed is big enough for this Jeff guy too*, she thought, laughing to herself, and shut down the tube to get some sleep. The silence of the room only made her thoughts of Jeff louder. Restless and craving the hottie she had just barely met, she closed her eyes, she pictured his hat backward now, almost falling off his head with his flowing brown hair touching her thighs, she imagined the heat and saturation of his tongue on her, in her, in and out. She lost herself in the fantasy of him now moving himself inside her, a purely sexual ache that she finally chased to an intense finish with her fingers. *Jeff, you feel so good*, she screamed as she climaxed.

It was the year two thousand and fourteen, and with technology on her side, Sasha turned to Facebook to hunt him down. She found him quickly: Jeff. His profile picture was a distant, arrogant shot of him, not even a headshot, and for the rest of his page, a total ghost town. He didn't post updates, ever; he didn't even acknowledge the "Happy Birthday" messages cluttering his wall from the previous December. He seemed like a man who used the platform to watch others rather than be seen, but that didn’t bother her; it actually intrigued her more. Because of his blatant arrogance, he had a phone number on the page, which was all Sasha needed. She typed the number into her phone, wanting to text him so badly, but realizing it was very late, she waited and saved the number in her contacts.

Awakening Saturday morning, Sasha had one thing, and only one thing on her mind, Jeff. So later that evening, she called him from a bar down the street to see if he wanted to catch a drink together. When he answered, his tone was clipped.

“Hey, this is Sasha. I met you last night at the bar. I know Jerry”.

"Yeah, I remember you," he said.

“You want to grab a drink together?” Sasha asked, bolstered by liquid courage.

“I just got home, I guess, meet me at the bar on East,” he said abruptly but playfully.

Sasha arrived first, sitting in her Suburban to steady her nerves, since Jerry and she split, she started doing more coke, always had it on her, bought at least once a week, it helped her focus on work. She snorted a line of coke. Looking in her rearview mirror, she sees a vehicle pull in right behind her and honk. In the twilight, she realized it was him, it was Jeff. A flicker of unease hit her. *How does he know what I drive? How does he know this is me?* But she quickly dismissed it, too blinded by the thrill that this super-hot guy actually wanted to catch a drink with her.

Sasha stepped out of her suburban, the coke humming in her veins, making her feel untouchable. She leaned into his window, her short black dress riding dangerously high.

"Hi, stranger," she purred.

Jeff didn't waste time on pleasantries. He looked her up and down with a predatory gaze and said,

"Forget this place. My house is around the corner. Let's go, follow me." Jeff said.

To Sasha, this felt like winning the lottery. She followed him to a house that looked like a cross between a trailer park home and a frat house after a rage. It was a mess, but in her state of mind and desire for this guy, she saw it as proof that no other woman lived there, which made her feel as if she would be his only, and she wanted to be his only.

Jeff grabbed them both beers from his fridge, and she reached into her purse,

"Hey, you want some shit, I got some," she said.

"Break out," Jeff says, grabbing a clean plate and a previously cut straw from the drawer.

He's not new to this, phew, she thought, relieved.

After some beers, lines, and laughs, Sasha was given the grand tour of the rathole he resided in. In the bedroom, a mattress lay on the floor, tangled in a tornado of sheets and pillows. She was slightly disgusted but also intrigued by the disaster he called home.

The tour ceased in the bedroom, which was, after all, the end of the house,

"Is this where you like to fuck, or just like to fuck yourself?", she playfully whispered to him.

Without notice, he grabbed her, wrapping her body into his arms, and kissed her hard on the lips, slipping his hands under her panties and into her. She was wet. They lay on the bed among the tornado of sheets, and he moved in and out of her, his hands on every inch of her tanned skin, his piercing blue eyes cutting right through her soul. Jeff stared into her eyes with the secure, confident passion that she had never seen before, for sure never in James and Jerry was lame in comparison to this hunk. The lovemaking was everything she had expected, everything she craved, and then some. They held each other for much of the night, as he snored her to sleep, but she barely slept, and she knew she had to go home; she felt as if, had she stayed longer, she would be smothering. Not wanting to suffocate him, she slipped away in the night while he slept, driving home with her skin still humming from the hot sex and lustful snuggling encounter, already obsessing over when she could feel him inside her again.

Sasha couldn't get Jeff's piercing blue eyes or his sun-bleached, light brown hair out of her head. He was a rugged vision of June sunshine, likely from his days working outdoors.

~~~

Early the next morning, Sasha had barely had enough sleep to recollect the evening, but sure and steady, her phone was ringing from a text, and she was waking up elated, even more so seeing that it was from Jeff;

JEFF: I woke up, and you were gone. I am making frittatas. Come over.

SASHA: Ok, gimme a few, and I will head over.

JEFF: Hurry up.

She was ecstatic. To her, this morning's after-sex call was deliberate,
~~~

signifying to her that it wasn't just a one-night stand; this was not the hook-up she thought it might be, quite unlike what should have stayed a hook-up with Jerry.

Even though his house had been a "pigsty" the night before, she thought he might have cleared the mountain of dishes from the sink. When she arrived, nothing had changed, but she didn't care. She sat at his kitchen island in a daze, watching him sauté mushrooms in butter. At thirty-four years old, tanned and fit at one hundred and thirty-five pounds, Sasha was a beautiful woman, but in Jeff's presence, she felt like a starstruck teenager, silenced by the sheer shock that a hottie like him actually wanted her, although, deeper, this was just a sure sign of her lack of esteem for herself.

Breakfast began romantically, Jeff's half-naked body slaving over the gas stove, wooing her about the night before, with butter sputtering onto his fit and tanned naked abdomen, he wore tight red underwear, and nothing else. It was phenomenally hot to Sasha, especially the way he was so confident with his body in front of her. The atmosphere shifted as Jeff cooked breakfast. He began questioning her about Jerry, his tone darkening as he insisted that they must still be together since they had gone out.

"I can see the way Jerry looks at you, though. He wants to fuck you still. You positive there's nothing going on there?" Jeff said, accusingly.

"Absolutely not, he and I are just friends literally. Just friends, we did date, but he wasn't for me," Sasha explained.

Sasha tried to explain they were just friends; the romance was dead but Jeff wasn't having it.

"It looks like more than that if you're still going out together," Jeff snapped.

Sasha was barely processing the warning signs; she was too distracted by his presence. She found herself agreeing with him, rationalizing that perhaps it did look bad to keep Jerry around. To please Jeff, she made a snap decision:

"I won't talk to him anymore. Jerry and I are done. I will prove it to you." Sasha pleaded.

...She was happy to let him take charge; she just wanted to feel him. She ached for his romance.

Jerry was a problem for another day. Or better yet, not a problem at all. To keep those blue eyes fixed on her like this, she would gladly drop Jerry into her past and never look back. She had won the prize, and she was going to keep it

CHAPTER 2: *The Illusion of Choice*

Jeff's expression softened into a satisfied smirk the moment she promised to cut ties with Jerry. As they ate their frittatas on the dark marbled granite island cluttered with unopened mail and crusty dishes, Sasha's mind was entirely elsewhere. She wasn't thinking about her soon-to-be-lost friendship; she was imagining Jeff grabbing her, sweeping the trash off the counter, and taking her right there. She was happy to let him take charge; she just wanted to feel him. She ached for his rugged brand of romance.

"That was so good, can I get dessert?" Sasha asked playfully, letting her clothes drop to the kitchen floor.

"Of course," Jeff said.

She boosted herself onto the kitchen island, offering no room for refusal. He raised his eyebrows, kneeling on the dirty floor as his tongue found her. Her moaning could have been heard miles away. Clutching his flowing, sun-kissed brown hair, his grip tight on her thighs, she pulled him up against her lips as he slid inside her. They climaxed together, a chaotic, breathless rush that left her skin humming.

~~~

The bubble burst a few days later. Sasha was sitting at her desk, trying to focus on editing a manuscript, when her phone buzzed with Jerry's name. She answered it sharply, hoping to end their communication quickly so she wouldn't have to deal with an awkward conversation.

"Sasha, thank God you answered," Jerry said, his voice breathless and frantic through the speaker. "Word travels fast around town. Someone saw you outside the East Street bar with Jeff. Look, I know things are dead between us, but you need to listen to me—Jeff is bad news. He's a textbook womanizer. He ruins every girl he touches."

To Sasha, it sounded like the desperate plea of an ex-lover losing his grip.

"Jeff is amazing, Jer," she shot back, her blood instantly boiling in defense. "He takes care of my needs; he's more of
~~~

a man than you could ever dream of being." She slammed the phone down, dismissing his warnings as pure envy. But Jerry didn't stop there. Frantic and losing control, he went behind her back, convincing her family to flag Jeff's reputation.

Sasha's phone rang later that evening, and on the other end of the line was her mother.

"Sasha, I heard about this Jeff character, Jerry said he's a womanizer, he said he knows him really well, and to stay away from him, he's into drugs and everything," Sasha's mother told her.

"Oh, Jerry's just jealous," Sasha said, playing it off. Ending the call with an attempt to convince her mother that she is fine and he is a good guy. Clearly, Sasha still didn't see a predator; she saw a man in high demand. The more they pushed, the tighter she pulled Jeff toward her. In her twisted reality, their frantic warning signs weren't red flags; they were proof that she won a competitive prize. A volatile mix of low self-esteem and the reckless, humming highs of the cocaine in her veins made her feel completely untouchable. She had escaped a dead marriage to James and a fractured, suffocating affair with Jerry. Jeff made her feel alive. If keeping his piercing blue eyes fixed on her meant cutting off the rest of the world, she would gladly seal herself inside his cage, step into his dark world, and call it a total victory.

CHAPTER 3: *Shattered Diamonds on the Dash*

The night was thick with the scent of lake water and the hum of a crowd. Sasha felt electric; she was on her home turf, walking into the only waterfront bar in the town with her prize man, Jeff, where the owners were old friends and the band was led by a guy she'd known since homeroom. With the residual buzz of her own excitement and a little chemical help, she felt like the queen of the town with the hottest man on earth with her. She wanted everyone to see her with Jeff, to know that he chose her. She wanted to show him off to the people who knew her for years, the ones that saw every floozy she dated before as deadbeats like James, proving to her long-time friends that she had finally found someone who matched her allure and intensity. Sasha had never chosen very good-looking guys in the past; Jeff was by far the most gorgeous one.

As they stepped inside, the music surged. Jeff headed towards the bar for drinks, not noticing that Sasha was waving to someone; she had spotted the lead singer, an old friend from high school, who was just stepping off the small stage for a break.

"Oh my god, hey!" she laughed, instinctively stepping forward to greet him.

“Sash, how the heck have you been?” The singer asked.

They shared a brief, sweaty, genuine hug, the kind of greeting shared by people who have decades of history. It was innocent, a flash of her old, popular, gregarious self. But when Sasha turned around, there stood Jeff staring at her with a look she had not yet seen from him; it didn’t even look like him. The air in the room seemed to drop twenty degrees. Jeff wasn't smiling. His blue eyes, usually so hypnotic, had turned into flat, dangerous chips of ice. He didn't greet the friend. He didn't even acknowledge the man's existence. He did not order the drinks. Instead, Jeff’s hand clamped onto Sasha’s upper arm not with the rough passion she craved in the bedroom, but with a cold, possessive weight that brooked no argument.

"We're leaving," he muttered, his voice a low vibration that only she could hear, though its jagged edge cut through the music.

"What? Jeff, but we just got here," Sasha pleaded.

"Now, Sasha," he hissed, his grip tightening just enough to signal his rising temper.

"What is wrong? What happened?" She asked, worried for him.

He didn't wait for her to say goodbye. He began to navigate her toward the exit like a piece of property he was reclaiming from a thief. From behind the polished wood of the bar, Coleen, the owner, watched the entire exchange. She had seen a thousand couples pass through these doors, but the way Jeff handled Sasha made her hair stand on end. She saw the way Sasha's initial confusion melted into a desperate, hurried compliance, her eyes darting to Jeff's face to gauge his anger. Coleen didn't see a "hottie" loving his woman; she saw a predator marking his territory and a friend who was already losing herself to the fog of a dangerous man. As the door swung shut behind them, Coleen felt a knot of dread tighten in her stomach. She knew that look, and she knew it never ended well.

The silence in the Suburban was suffocating as Sasha pulled out of the parking lot. The adrenaline from the bar had curdled into a sharp, cold anxiety. Jeff sat in the passenger seat, his profile stony and dark in the glow of the dashboard lights.

"You’re a real piece of work, aren't you?" he spat suddenly, his voice dripping with contempt. "We go to a bar, and you immediately throw yourself at some old flame? You dragged me there just so you could play the slut in front of your old boyfriend?" Jeff said angrily.

Sasha’s heart hammered against her ribs.

"Jeff, no! He’s just an old friend, I swear," she argued, her voice trembling but desperate to fix the mood.

She reached out to touch his arm, trying to bring back the man who had made her frittatas and looked at her with those piercing blue eyes, and made love to her like no other ever had. In her mind, this wasn't abuse; it was passion. His jealousy made it seem like he cared about her and desired her. Sasha wanted to be desired by him; she wanted him to want her. She told herself that his rage was just proof of how much he wanted her, a sign that he was so deeply in love that the mere thought of another man touching her drove him mad. She felt a twisted sense of importance; she was the only woman who could provoke this much fire in a man like him.

"Don't lie to me!" Jeff roared, the sound filling the cramped cabin of the Suburban.

Sasha started to protest again, her words coming out in a frantic rush, but she was cut short by the sound of glass splintering in front of her.

Jeff hadn't hit her. Instead, he lunged forward, his fist a blur of controlled fury as he punched his hand straight through the windshield of her Chevy Suburban. The safety glass shattered into a thousand glittering diamonds, a spiderweb of cracks blooming outward from the impact of his knuckles. Sasha froze, slamming on the brakes as glass rained down onto the dashboard and her lap. She was in shock, at first thinking that something had hit it, but she knew it was Jeff; he did this, he acted out in such a way that caused something that she had never seen broken to this extent before, to become broken.

The violence was so sudden, so raw, that it left her breathless. He sat there, chest heaving, his hand still pressed against the jagged ruins of the glass. In the terrifying silence that followed, Sasha didn't see the danger. She saw a man who was so all-in on her that he was willing to break himself and her car just to express his agony. She looked at the shattered glass and, through the haze of fear and the lingering high of the night, she saw it as a monument to his love.

The force of the shattered glass was followed by a silence so heavy it felt like it was crushing the oxygen out of the vehicle. Jeff didn't look at her. He didn't check whether she was cut. He just sat there, his knuckles bleeding, and stared through the spiderwebbed ruins of the windshield.

"Jeff, I'm so sorry, I didn't mean—" Sasha begged.

"Just take me home," he interrupted, his voice flat and icy.

The blame was unspoken but absolute.

He made her feel as though her "betrayal" had forced his hand, as if she were the one who had reached out and smashed the glass herself.

When they pulled into his darkened driveway, the panic in Sasha's chest reached a fever pitch. She couldn't let him go inside angry; she couldn't handle the thought of him retracting his love.

"Please, let me come in," she pleaded to him, reaching for him through the glittering dust of the safety glass. "Let me stay. I'll make it up to you, I promise. I never wanted to make you feel this way." She begged.

Jeff didn't offer a word of comfort. He simply unbuckled the seatbelt, stepped out of the car, and slammed the door with such force that the cracked windshield groaned. He vanished into the house, leaving Sasha alone in a wrecked car, trembling with a guilt that wasn't hers to carry.

The drive back to her house was a blur of tears, but the moment she walked through her door, her phone began to scream with texts. The notifications were a relentless barrage, a calculated mix of love-bombing and "slut-shaming" designed to keep her spinning.

JEFF: I really thought you were the one.

The first text read.

JEFF: I never loved anyone until you, and you just broke me tonight. You destroyed us.

Sasha's thumbs flew across the screen, her heart breaking.

SASHA: I love you too! I'm so sorry, Jeff. It didn't mean anything; please believe me.

But the mask slipped again instantly. The next wave of texts was a vicious pivot.

JEFF: You're probably high right now, aren't you? He typed, weaponizing her drug use against her.

JEFF: I bet you've got someone else there.

You've been cheating on me since the day we met.

You're just a lying, high-school-peaked junkie. Sasha stared at the screen, her vision swimming. One minute, he was the man who loved her more than anyone, and the next, he was a judge sentencing her for crimes she hadn't committed. Instead of seeing the cruelty, Sasha felt a desperate, addictive need to prove her innocence. She was hooked on the version of him that loved her, and she was willing to endure the version of him that hated her just to get it back.

Sasha stared at the glowing screen of her phone; the vitriol of Jeff's texts reflected in her eyes. One minute, he was the man who loved her more than anyone, and the next, he was a judge sentencing her for crimes she hadn't committed. Instead of seeing the cruelty, Sasha felt a desperate, addictive need to prove her innocence. She was hooked on the version of him that loved her, and she was willing to endure the version of him that hated her just to get it back.

~~~

She didn't sleep. By morning, the silence was broken by a single text. No apology, no explanation, just a transactional olive branch.

JEFF: I'm giving you the money for the windshield. Come get the check. The door is open.

Relief washed over her so fast it made her dizzy. She convinced herself that this was his way of saying sorry without bruising his massive ego. She drove over immediately, the morning wind whistling through the jagged cracks in her windshield, a constant reminder of the violence she was already preparing to overlook.

When she stepped inside, the frat house chaos of the day before had been swallowed by a heavy, artificial night. The blinds were drawn tight, sealing the small house in a tomb of shadows. Sasha navigated the cramped hallway toward
~~~

the bedroom, her heart skipping as she pushed open the door.

Jeff was a silhouette against the rumpled sheets, his naked body catching a singular, sharp sliver of light that bled through the edge of the blinds. He didn't speak. He just turned those piercing blue eyes toward her, radiating a quiet, magnetic heat. He looked vulnerable, yet entirely in control. Any lingering anxiety Sasha had felt vanished, replaced by a visceral, heavy pull in her gut. She fell for the sweetness of his silence, desperate to wash the terror of the night before away.

When he asked her to get on her knees, she did it without a second thought. She poured all her love, her apologies, and her compliance into him, swallowing the shame, believing this was how she bought her way back into his good graces.

"I have to get going," she whispered eventually, pulling herself away from the heat of the bed, the heat of his naked hot body.

“Your check is on the island in the kitchen,” Jeff muttered, turning his back to her.

She dressed quietly, feeling a twisted sense of satisfaction. She was back in his favor. The storm had passed.

Sasha walked out into the kitchen, the dim light making the mess on the counter look like a jagged landscape. She snatched the check, but as she pulled her hand back, her eyes snagged on a small cluster of items tucked beside the stack of unopened mail.

A tarnished, bent silver spoon with chalky white residue caked in the bowl. A flick-style lighter. A bright orange box of baking soda.

She froze, her breath catching in her throat. She knew coke, she knew the social energy and the fun bar time high, the high that helped her focus on her editing work. But this setup was different. This looked industrial, dirty, and desperate.

The hypocrisy hit her like a physical blow, cracking through her denial with a sickening clarity. Just hours ago, Jeff had been blowing up her phone, calling her a junkie and a slut, shaming her for the lines she took to feel confident. And all the while, he was standing over his stove, cooking crack. He had sat in that dark bedroom, playing the wounded, heartbroken lover, letting her degrade herself on her knees for him, while he was coming down from a hit of something that destroyed lives.

An oily, degrading feeling coated her skin. She wasn't a prize to him. She was just an audience member in his wreckage.

She ran out to her Suburban, slamming the door so hard the cracked windshield groaned. Her hands shook so violently she could barely type, the residual cocaine from the night before turning her blood into pure rage. Her thumbs flew across the screen.

SASHA: I saw what was on your counter, Jeff. The spoon, the soda. I'm not stupid. You have a lot of nerve calling me a junkie when you're literally cooking crack in your kitchen. You made me get on my knees for you while you were high on that shit? You're disgusting.

SASHA: Don't bother responding. You're a hypocrite and a jerk, and I am completely done.

She threw the phone onto the passenger seat and slammed her hands against the steering wheel, finally breaking into ugly, violent tears. For the first time since meeting him, the gorgeous hunk didn't look like a prize. He looked like a monster. And as she looked through the spiderwebbed glass of her truck, she realized she had just cut off her friends, her ex, and her family, all to stand completely alone in a dynamic she didn't understa

CHAPTER 4: *The Hundo*

With Jeff silenced by her final text, Sasha felt a physical weight lift. The handsome devil was behind her, and the annual town carnival was ahead, a neon-soaked tradition that signaled the height of summer.

This was Sasha's element. She didn't want to sit at home brooding over shattered glass and kitchen-counter chemistry; she wanted the smell of fried dough, the thumping bass of the midway, and the company of people who actually appreciated her.

She decided to reach out to Jerry, extending a calculated olive branch. She knew he'd be there, and she knew he'd be looking for a way to sharpen the night's edge. Sasha had always been the one who could fix things for her friends; she had the connections and the confidence to move a little product without breaking a sweat. To her, it wasn't about the money; it was about being the life of the party, the person everyone relied on to make the night legendary. It proved that she was still the brilliant, popular girl who could multitask better than anyone.

She messaged Jerry,

SASHA: Hey, I'm heading to the carnival. Meet me by the Ferris wheel at eight. Bringing the good stuff.

Jerry was hesitant after her recent disappearance into Jeff's world, but the lure of the fix Sasha promised was too much to resist.

JERRY: I suppose we could meet you there. I am going with my cousin. I'll grab some from you. But dude, you better watch out for that asshole, if he's around, we're out.

Sasha smirked. She assumed Jeff's silence meant she'd won, that he was too ashamed of his secret cooking to face her.

~~~

As the sun began to dip below the horizon, painting the New York sky in bruised purples and oranges, the carnival lights flickered to life. Sasha walked out of her house, walking past her shiny suburban with a repaired windshield paid for with Jeff's guilt check, glinting in the twilight. She felt like a winner. She
~~~

had the money, the gear, and her friends back.

As she stepped into the humid night air, wandering among the cars that lined the festival grounds to get to the carnival grounds, she didn't see the dark truck parked three rows back, its engine off and its driver watching her every move through the glass.

The air at the carnival was thick with the smell of fried dough and the mechanical hum of the Ferris wheel spinning against the night sky. Sasha walked through the midway, the neon lights reflecting off the asphalt, trying to lose herself in the noise. But her pocket buzzed a persistent, rhythmic vibration that cut through the music.

It was Jeff. The rage from his texts the week before was entirely gone, replaced by a tone that was eerily calm.

JEFF: Hey, Sash, are you at the carnival? He texted.

He was testing her, waiting for a lie he could use against her later. Sasha didn't blink.

SASHA: I'm at the carnival. What's up?

JEFF: You got any shit? His next message read.

Sasha paused near the game booths. The business side of her brain clicked on. If he wanted to buy, she could make a quick profit, and a part of her, the part still addicted to those blue eyes, she figured it might lead to a makeup session that would smooth over the crack-pipe discovery. But the memory of the shattered windshield was still a cold weight in her stomach. She was leery, her instincts humming a warning that the fun was curdling into something else. Then the next text came in.

Jeff: I'm at your house.

A chill ran down her spine. The fairgrounds were directly across the street from her place; she had walked over, leaving her truck in the driveway as a beacon. He wasn't just reaching out; he was occupying her space.

SASHA: I'm meeting friends, she typed back.

JEFF: We need to talk. I'm really upset, Sasha...

JEFF: I need to see you. Please.

The heavy, manipulative gravity of his words pulled at her. Sasha felt the old familiar tug of loyalty and a dangerous curiosity that had gotten her into this mess. She pulled up her thread with Jerry, the friend she had promised to meet, and sent a quick, clipped text:

SASHA: Going to be late. Change of plans, I'll text you.

~~~

She turned away from the bright lights and the safety of the crowd, walking back across the street toward her darkened driveway. As Sasha turned the corner, the neon glow of the carnival faded, replaced by the dim yellow of her porch light.

Jeff was sitting on the front steps, his head in his hands. He looked small, shrunken, and defeated. The relief that washed over her was almost intoxicating; he wasn't the windshield-smashing predator from the week before. He was just a man who had been broken by the world.

She approached him cautiously, but the moment she reached the steps, he reached out. His touch was ghost-light on her arm, a gentle, pleading contact that
~~~

made her previous rage feel suddenly cruel.

"Sasha," he rasped, his voice thick with emotion. "My brother fired me today. It's over, I'm done."

"What? Jeff, what happened?" she asked, her fixer instincts immediately taking over. Jeff didn't answer. He just looked up at her with glassy, watery blue eyes, as if he were on the verge of tears. He needed her. Her power rushed back into her veins.

She led him inside, the tension of the crack-pipe discovery buried under the immediate need to soothe him. Taking care of someone meant providing the best, and in her world, that often meant a high-quality line.

She laid it out on the glass table, meticulously cutting a line of coke for him. She reached into her wallet and pulled out a crisp, stiff hundred-dollar bill. She had always been fastidious about the fact that singles were dirty, handled by a thousand hands, but a hundred-dollar bill felt cleanly elite. It felt like her.

Jeff stared at the bill, a predatory spark momentarily replacing the sadness in his eyes.

"A hundo?" A sexy grin finally broke through his depressed facade. He looked up at her with a flash of the old, arrogant Jeff she was addicted to. "That's my girl."

Jeff settled onto her sofa, the hundo still clutched in his hand, his eyes tracking her every move. When Sasha mentioned she had to head back to the carnival because Jerry was waiting, the atmosphere froze. Jeff didn't blow up or punch a wall. Instead, let out a long, ragged sigh that sounded like a man at the end of his rope.

“Do you know how many knots are in a noose?” he asked, his eyes turning dead and grim

She stopped breathing.

"You're really going to leave me tonight?" he asked, his voice low and wounded. "After I lost my job, my brother fired me, Sasha. I thought you were the one person who actually gave a shit about me. Don’t go back there. Stay here. I want you all to myself tonight. I need you."

He used his sorrow as bait, then his body to set the hook. He began to kiss her with a desperate, frantic intensity, making her feel like her presence was the only thing keeping him alive. It was a beautiful, intoxicating performance of need.

The texts from Jerry started to chime on the coffee table, but Jeff's hand was already sliding up her thigh, his blue eyes locked onto hers with a pleading heat. He was rewarding her for staying, feeding her the intimacy she craved as a payment for her isolation.

Sasha silenced her phone, tossing it aside. The thrill of the carnival and the money she could have made seemed small compared to the massive ego-stroke of being Jeff's savior.

The next morning, she woke up bathed in the glow of Jeff's newfound ambition. He wasn't the defeated man from the night before; he was energized, his blue eyes sharp with an infectious vision.

"I'm done working for my brother's scraps," he said, confidently, as they sat in her quiet kitchen. "I've got the experience. I've got the tools. I know the business better than anyone in this town; my brother learned from me. It's time I started my own HVAC business."

He leaned in close, making her feel like the most important partner in the world.

"What do you think? You're the smart one, Sasha. You've got the head for this. Do you think I could make it work?"

A rush of pride flooded her chest. After years of being with a deadbeat, like James, here was a man with a plan, a man who recognized her brilliance. They were becoming a power couple.

"I've got everything I need except the wheels," Jeff admitted, his tone turning humble again. "I can't haul my equipment in an old, rusted-out car. I need a van to get this off the ground. If you could help me, get the van, Sasha... we'd be unstoppable. I'd be doing this for us." He pleaded with her.

He framed it perfectly. It wasn't a handout; it was an investment in their shared future.

A small, quiet voice in the back of Sasha's mind flickered to life, reminding her of the shattered windshield, the dark room, and the silver spoon on the counter. They had hit some incredibly rough patches for a couple who had barely begun. She hesitated, her hand hovering over the metaphorical trigger of her bank account.

But as she looked at him, he was rugged, experienced, and seemingly devoted. He was a genius at wiring commercial units. He was talented. He was a hard worker when he wanted to be. With his skills and her backing, he'd be pulling in contracts and paying her back before the first oil change.

"Okay," she said, the word feeling like a heavy seal on their new contract. "Let's get the van."

The transformation in Jeff was instantaneous. He showered her with gratitude, making her feel like a visionary. She felt a surge of maternal pride mixed with sexual heat; she was the woman who saved him when his own family wouldn't. Once the business was running, the messy parts of Jeff, the bad drugs, the temper would simply evaporate under the pressure of a steady paycheck.

She poured her hard-earned savings into a used white work van. Driving it home, it felt like a tangible, heavy anchor. To Sasha, it was a beautiful symbol of their future together. She smiled, completely blind to the fact that she had just handed a predator the keys to his own freedom, trading her hard-earned independence to become the permanent enabler of his sinking ship.

CHAPTER 5: *Digital Keys*

The timing was too perfect to be an accident. Just days after Jeff had been working under the hood of her suburban, claiming he was checking the fluids, Sasha pulled out of his driveway only to hear the sickening, metallic scream of her transmission shredding itself.

The transmission was entirely blown. Suddenly, she was stranded, forced to rely on Jeff and the very van she had just bought for him. She has no wheels of her own.

Jeff, ever the hero, had an immediate solution: he'd sell her his old car. It was a massive lateral move, but at least she'd be mobile. Sasha took the deal, desperate to keep her life on track.

A week later, the illusion collapsed. Sasha took her new ride into the shop for a desperately required oil change. She got the car home from the shop, got cleaned up, and was heading out to see Jeff. While still in her driveway, Sasha turned the key. Instead of the steady hum of an engine, the car belched a thick, suffocating cloud of gray smoke that blanketed the driveway. Panicked, she called Jeff, her voice trembling as she described the mechanical heart failure of the vehicle he had just sold her.

"Jeff, something is seriously wrong with this car. It's billowing white smoke. I think it's the engine, it's dead."

The response wasn't sweet or helpful. Jeff's voice turned into a jagged blade.

"Oh, so now you're accusing me of selling you a piece of junk? After everything I've done to help you?" his rage crackled through the phone speaker. "You probably drove it out of oil and fried the motor, Sasha. How could you be that careless?"

Sasha stood in the driveway, the smell of burnt oil clinging to her hair, and felt a wave of profound shame. Jeff sounded so certain, so righteously indignant, that her own memory began to blur. She was supposed to be the smart one, the achiever, yet here she was, apparently failing at the basic task of maintaining a vehicle.

"I... I just got an oil change," she stammered.

Jeff hung up, leaving her in the silence of the smoke.

She knew deep down that billowing white smoke meant a blown head gasket. Yet, standing in the wreckage of her independence, her confidence fractured. She felt utterly convinced that she was the one who had failed. She was exactly where he wanted her: stranded, broke, and apologetic for a crime she didn't commit.

By that evening, the reality of the investment began to set in. With her car gone and the van now their only means of transport, Sasha was effectively grounded. A nagging sense of guilt tugged at her, the brilliant part of her brain trying to scream that she had made a massive mistake, but she suppressed it. Jeff didn't offer any financial solutions. Instead, he seemed to thrive in his newfound role as her gatekeeper. He was the one with the keys. He was the one who decided where she went and when she got home.

On the drive back to his house, the mask of the professional businessman slipped completely. Jeff didn't bother hiding his habits anymore. He picked up a massive handle of vodka, and by the time they reached his backyard, the ambition of the morning had dissolved into a familiar, hazy decadence.

They sat in his small, fenced-in yard, a claustrophobic space choked with weeds and the trunk of a fallen tree. Jeff gestured to the dead wood with his glass.

"It's black walnut," he bragged, his speech starting to slur. "Highly desirable. I'm going to mill it down, make tables out of it. It's worth a fortune."

Sasha watched him, wanting so badly to believe in his talent. Between drinks, they sat on their phones, taking photos of each other and laughing, a desperate attempt to capture the fun she still believed they could have. He talked big about the business, claiming he was slammed with work, and asked her to take over the billing and invoicing.

"I hate paperwork, Sash. I need your brain for that." She agreed, ignoring the fact that he hadn't paid a single dime toward the van yet, outside of deducting the cost of the busted car he sold her. She needed him to be successful because if he wasn't, she was just a woman stuck in a weed-choked yard with a drunk.

The night blurred into a drunken fog on the couch, ending only when Jeff finally passed out, leaving his phone face-up on the kitchen counter.

The next morning, the sunlight was unforgiving, highlighting every bit of grime in the house. Sasha stood in the kitchen, her head throbbing as she started to fix breakfast. She wasn't trying to be nosy; she didn't want to be *that* woman. But as the screen of Jeff's phone lit up with a notification, her eyes locked onto it.

The messages weren't about HVAC contracts or black walnut tables. They were pings from a dating app.

The man who had *needed* her all to himself, the man who was using her money and her van to rebuild his life, was still scrolling for his next hit. The sweet Jeff who had cried on her front steps was gone. In his place was the cold, calculating hunter. Sasha stood in the kitchen, realizing she had personally paid for the very wheels he was using to find her replacement.

When Jeff woke up, she demanded the truth, she didn't shrink away. Her old confidence flared. But Jeff didn't even bother to argue; he simply snatched the phone and retreated into the bathroom, clicking the lock. It was a cowardly, silent wall that left Sasha standing in the hallway, fuming.

When he finally emerged, his face was a mask of bored innocence.

"It's an old app, Sasha. Old messages," he said, waving it off like it was a technical glitch. "I don't even know how to shut the account down."

It was a weak lie, and they both knew it.

Sasha chose to believe it only because the alternative, that she was completely stranded and being played, was too humiliating to swallow. But the seed was planted. She wasn't just a doting girlfriend anymore; she was on high alert.

The dynamic shifted quickly from business partners to a grim dictatorship.

Jeff didn't want her brilliant input; he wanted a servant. He barked orders at her, telling her to hurry up and get it done, while she sat hunched over his messy billing records. He treated her like trash, a far cry from the woman who had once been the most popular girl in the room.

The isolation became entirely physical. When she finally finished his paperwork and begged him to pick her up from her place, longing for the reward of his presence, he turned cold.

"I'm too tired to drive," he muttered over the phone. "If you can get here, come over. I'm just chilling, having a few drinks out back." He told her.

He knew she was stuck. He kept her in a state of perpetual waiting, like a bird in a cage, visiting her only when he was bored.

When Jeff's phone went dark a few days later, he blamed the carrier, spinning a yarn about bad service and billing errors. He proposed they get a joint plan, a move he framed as a sign of commitment, but it was really just another way to get Sasha to foot the bill.

She obliged, adding his phone to her account. It was a fatal mistake on his part, though, unbeknownst to him at the time. Jeff saw a free phone plan; Sasha saw a dashboard. She was smart, smarter than he gave her credit for. She knew that as the primary account holder, she held the digital keys.

Late one night, she logged into the carrier dashboard. Her eyes scanned the call logs, the timestamps jumping out at her like neon warning signs. He was making calls and sending texts at two o'clock and three o'clock in the morning, when he claimed to be fast asleep, hours when she wasn't with him. She began to Google the numbers, her stomach dropping as name after name appeared: women from the area, women with active dating profiles, even one she knew from the bars.

The *old app* lies disintegrated. She was paying for the data he used to hunt, and for the first time, Sasha wasn't just angry, she was armed.

Sasha played the part of the devoted girlfriend, but inside, she was a storm of ice and rage. She knew she couldn't rock the boat yet. Without a car of her own, Jeff was her only physical tether to the outside world, and she refused to be completely stranded. Instead, she became a ghost in his digital life. She began printing the call logs, timestamps, and names, creating a secret, physical archive of his betrayal.

Then came the jackpot. Using her knowledge of his lazy habits, she guessed his dating app password. The exact same password he used for his work email. When the screen finally loaded, Sasha's heart turned over. There were the messages: the plans, the flirting, the lies. She looked at the photos of the other woman. *Not even as pretty as I am*, she whispered to the empty room, a flicker of her old ego providing a small, bitter shield against the jealousy that was eating her alive.

The following Friday morning felt like a funeral. They had just spent the night together, sex that felt more like a demeaning chore than an act of passion. As the morning light began to creep through the blinds, Jeff's phone on the bed erupted.

Buzz. Buzz. Buzz.

At seven o'clock in the morning, the vibration sounded like a siren in the quiet room. Jeff didn't move a muscle, but Sasha saw his jaw tighten. He reached out, his hand fumbling in the dark to flip the phone face down, silencing the caller without looking at the screen. He went back to pretending he was asleep, his breathing too heavy, too forced. Sasha lay beside him, her eyes wide open, memorizing the exact second the phone had gone off.

~~~

The moment she was back at her place, she logged into the account. Her hands were perfectly steady as she scrolled through the data usage from that morning.

There it was. An incoming call was timestamped at exactly seven that morning.

She cross-referenced the number with the messages she had copied from the dating app. It was a perfect match.
~~~

The woman from the dating app was calling Jeff while he was still lying in bed with Sasha. The evidence was no longer just a suspicion; it was a map of his double life.

Sasha stared at the computer screen, the secret printouts piling up in a hidden folder beside her. She was trapped in his grasp, but she was slowly building a cage of her own one made of paper, data, and the cold, hard truth.

Chapter 6: *Playing the Losing Hand*

Over the following weeks, Jeff became a ghost in his own life, remaining distant and cold. But while he was absent from her bed, he was a permanent fixture at the bar where they had first met. Sasha began walking down to her own local spot, a solitary, quiet trek that felt like a penance. Inside, the air was thick with gossip. Her friends, nursing their drinks, didn't hold back. They saw through Jeff's busy businessman act; they saw a man who spent more time at the bottom of a glass than on a job site. Sasha listened, her heart a tangled mess of jealousy and denial. She knew they were right, but the fire of her obsession hadn't burned out yet. She wasn't ready to let go; she was desperate to own him.

While at the bar, the resourceful version of Sasha finally made a move. After scrolling through listings at a used car lot outside of town, she found a vehicle cheap enough to buy outright. She refused to be a prisoner to Jeff's schedule any longer. She enlisted a friend to drive her to the lot, determined to claim any cheap set of wheels that could get her from point A to point B. She walked away with a used Honda Element. It was boxy, utilitarian, and in her eyes utterly hideous. It was a far cry from the sleek, popular image she loved to project. But it was hers. It was good on gas, and more importantly, it was a getaway vehicle.

The dealership sat directly adjacent to the bar where her life had first collided with Jeff's. As she hopped out of her friend's car to claim her new keys, she saw it: the white van sitting idle in the gravel lot.

It was three o'clock in the afternoon on a workday. Jeff should have been running commercial estimates, but the van sat completely still. Seeing it there, while she was literally bumming rides just to gain an ounce of freedom, made her blood run cold. He was inside, likely spending the money she had helped him make, while she was humbling herself in a hideous used car just to survive. She gripped the keys to the Honda, the plastic edges digging deep into her palm.

Sasha stood by her new-to-her car, her hands trembling. The sight of that van was a silent scream of betrayal. She pulled out her phone and fired off a text, sharp and cold:

SASHA: Nice seeing you at the bar today.

The reply came back almost instantly, dripping with toxic venom.

JEFF: Oh, were you in the parking lot sucking CJ off again?

The words hit her like a physical blow. The sheer audacity of it, accusing her of a lewd, public act with a local regular while he sat in a tavern on her dime made her vision go blurry with rage.

SASHA: You're the cheat and the liar, not me, asshole.

She was on fire. Part of her wanted to storm across the pavement, burst through the dim tavern doors, and humiliate him in front of whoever he was sitting with. But the old popular girl insecurities crawled up her throat. She was terrified of what she might find. Was he with one of the women from the app? Would she walk in only to be mocked and labeled the crazy desperate girlfriend?

The fear of losing face won out over her fury. She couldn't give him the satisfaction of a scene, not yet. She climbed into the boxy cabin of the Honda Element, the smell of old plastic upholstery mocking her, and she drove back toward the safety of her neighborhood.

She didn't go home to cool off. Instead, she headed straight to the bar down the road to meet Syrena. Syrena had been a fixture in Sasha's life since the end of her relationship with Jerry. A whirlwind of a woman whose own emotional struggles made her a chaotic, yet somehow comforting, companion. Syrena didn't offer grounded advice; she offered a mirror to Sasha's own spiraling emotions.

When Syrena asked for a fix, Sasha realized she was dry. The constant drama with Jeff had drained her of everything, including her stash. She made a quick, clipped call. Ten minutes later, a car rolled through the dark end of the lot, a quick exchange was made, and the night shifted gears.

With the chemicals hitting her system, Sasha felt the jagged edges of her nerves begin to sharpen into a weapon. Syrena sat beside her under the neon beer signs, her eyes wide and humming with a manic energy.

"He's just like me, Sasha," Syrena said, her voice a mix of warning and thrill. "The moods, the blow-ups... he's bipolar as hell."

Sasha didn't argue. She knew the unpredictable weather patterns she dealt with in Syrena were the exact same ones she was addicted to in Jeff.

Sasha had been the it-girl, the brilliant student, the popular heartbreaker. She had never been the one left behind in the dust. She didn't just want Jeff; she wanted the satisfaction of being the one to bury the relationship. She wanted to be the executioner, not the victim. She was always the one who dumped the guy, and she wasn't going to lose her pride now.

"You need to tell him to his face," Syrena urged. "Let's go. It's just up the road. No big deal."

Sasha gripped the steering wheel of the Honda. Fueled by the drugs and Syrena's thirst for a fight, Sasha threw the car into gear. Syrena was a legendary fighter in their circles, ready to tear Jeff apart for what he'd done to her girl.

They sped down the dark country road, Sasha's stomach a violent knot of nerves, anger, and a sick, lingering passion. But with Syrena beside her, she felt invincible. She wasn't walking in as the *crazy girlfriend* anymore. She was walking in with a bodyguard and a heart full of cold, hard data.

When the heavy wooden door swung open, the powder keg Sasha expected to explode didn't. Instead, the bar was a scene of mundane, small-town comfort. Jeff was there, leaned back with a Labatt Blue, casually chatting with a regular. No side-chicks, no whispers, no drama. The wind was instantly sucked out of Syrena's sails; she looked disappointed, her fighter's adrenaline left with nowhere to go.

Sasha felt her own rage dissolve into a confusing, shaky relief. As they approached, Jeff gave her that nod, that slow, effortless upward tilt of his head that was both a greeting and a claim. It was the look that made her heart melt, and her body ache for him all at once. Despite the printed logs in her bag and the thousands she'd spent on his van, she was completely paralyzed by that blue-eyed gaze.

Syrena watched the transformation with bitter, mounting frustration, seeing Sasha's weakness unfold like a silk sheet, for a man who didn't deserve it. For Syrena, the frustration ran even deeper; she had always joked that the song "Girl Crush" was her anthem for Sasha, a serenade of obsession that skipped the jealousy of the man and went straight to the infatuation with her gorgeous and brilliant friend. Seeing Sasha reduce herself to a yes-girl for a deadbeat in a baseball cap was more than Syrena could stand.

Jeff played it cool, claiming he'd had an early start to the day and was heading home. When Sasha mentioned the Honda, he smirked.

"I already heard. Townies talk."

To Sasha, it felt like he was paying attention, like he actually cared.

The CJ accusation wasn't even mentioned; it had just been a weapon Jeff used to keep her defensive, now that she was standing in front of him, soft and eager, he didn't need the weapon anymore.

He declined her offer of company with a flat,

"I'm tired," Jeff said, but he made sure to give her a list of chores.

"I'll drop off the paperwork tomorrow," he said, already treating her like a clerk again. "And would you mind coming by sometime this week? My place is a mess. I need you to clean up and do some laundry."

"Sure," Sasha replied, her voice easy and compliant. She had gone from a private investigator with a file of evidence to a maid in the span of five minutes.

Back at Sasha's house, the night wound down with the familiar hum of coke and cold drinks. Sasha and Syrena sat out on the warm summer night, gazing up at the stars, trying to hold on to the silence. Syrena sat beside her, stunned into a rare quiet by how easily Sasha had folded. Sasha felt the high of the drugs and the lingering heat of Jeff's nod, completely ignoring the fact that she was currently paying for his phone, paying for his van, and was now scheduled to scrub his floors while he continued to message women.

The next morning, the sunlight hitting Sasha's desk felt like an interrogation. She was worn out, her skin pale, and her nerves frayed from the chemicals. When Jeff appeared to drop off the invoices, he didn't offer a hug or a coffee; he offered a smirk.

"Too many bumps last night?" he asked, his voice dripping with judgment.

"Whatever, Jeff," Sasha snapped, her exhaustion sharpening her tongue. "What's actually been going on? You've been too busy to see me, too many other dates on that app?"

Jeff didn't flinch. He played the martyr perfectly.

"I told you, I'm not seeing anyone. Not even you. I loved you, Sasha, but you haven't been there for me."

"Haven't been there for you?" Sasha's voice rose, incredulous. "I bought you a van! You left me with no wheels and a phone bill full of future hookups while I'm the one paying for it!"

"I have never cheated on you," he lied, his blue eyes wide and deceptively earnest. "You were the only love I ever had."

Dropping the stack of invoices on her desk like a burden he was passing off, he walked out, wearing a look of staged heartbreak that left Sasha questioning her own sanity.

The next day, Sasha was at his house anyway, fulfilling her duty. She did his laundry, folding the clothes she had paid to help him keep clean, and moved through the small, cramped rooms with a duster. There were no stray hairpins, no scent of perfume. For a moment, she felt a flicker of hope. Maybe he was telling the truth.

Then, she reached up to the high TV stand, her fingers searching for dust in the shadows above her head. She heard a light, rhythmic clink-clink as something began to roll. She reached further, her hand closing around a small, cold object.

It was a used glass pipe.

Sasha stood frozen in the middle of his living room, staring at the burnt residue on the glass. The realization hit her with a sickening thud. He wasn't necessarily dating the women on the app; he was likely hunting for a score or a high. He hadn't been ignoring her for another woman; he was ignoring her for the pipe. She didn't scream. She didn't break it. She simply placed it back in the shadows, tucked away like a secret she wasn't supposed to know.

She stayed. She finished the cleaning, the smell of bleach masking the rot of the relationship, and sat on his couch to wait. She wanted to be there when he got home, to be the good girl who had cleaned his house.

Hours passed. The house grew dark. Finally, she texted him.

SASHA: Where are you?

JEFF: The bar.

SASHA: I'm at your place. Everything is cleaned. I want to see you.

JEFF: Gonna be a while.

The rejection was flat and final. Without Syrena there to fuel her rage, Sasha sat alone in the silence of the house she had just scrubbed for him. She realized he wasn't coming. Eventually, she stood up, grabbed her keys to the Honda, and drove home through the dark. She told herself that if she just gave him space, if she didn't stalk him or nag him, he would eventually remember how much he loved her and come back around. She was playing a losing hand, hoping her silence would finally save them.

CHAPTER 7: *Apologies for Memories*

By late August, the humid air felt as stagnant as Sasha's life. When Jeff texted her to meet him at the bar, she didn't hesitate. She was tethered to him by a suffocating web of debt, the van, the phone plan, the business investment. She convinced herself she had to stay close to protect her assets, using logic to mask the primal, addictive pull she still felt every time he looked at her. But when she arrived at the tavern, the ambitious businessman was gone. Jeff was three sheets to the wind, his eyes completely glazed over and his coordination shot.

Sasha left her Honda Element in the gravel lot and climbed into the driver's seat of the white work van, chauffeuring her own debtor back to her house. As she hurried inside to grab an overnight bag, planning to play the doting caretaker at his place, Jeff sat in the passenger seat, scrolling through her phone under the guise of *playing music*.

The peace was shattered by a sharp, plastic crack.

While Sasha gathered her things in the house, Jeff's wandering eyes had navigated into her cloud storage. He had unearthed photos from a lifetime ago, intimate, playful shots of her and Jerry that she hadn't looked at in years.

In a drunken, jealous fit, Jeff didn't just yell. He took the phone in both hands and twisted it with brute force until the screen and the internal circuits snapped. He hurled the two broken pieces into a muddy puddle in the yard and stormed toward the house, nearly taking Sasha out with the screen door as he bolted past her. He was a whirlwind of irrational rage.

"Whore, I saw your photos. You're fucking Jerry." He screamed, charging back out of the house, stomping down the street into the deepening dusk.

Sasha, desperate and confused, fished the ruined device out of the mud. She climbed into the van and followed him down the road, rolling down the window to plead for an explanation. Jeff met her with a solid wall of silence, his face a mask of pure, unadulterated hate. There was clearly no reasoning with him.

She drove to the phone store, her hands shaking violently on the wheel. The clerk behind the counter looked at the mangled phone, muddy hardware, then up at the beautiful, distressed woman standing in front of him.

"Wow, someone got angry," he said, his voice blunt and honest.

Sasha barely heard him. She didn't want small talk; she just wanted Jeff. She paid out of pocket for the immediate replacement, her mind racing with a desperate need to find him and make sure he was alright, as if he were somehow the victim of the night's violence.

When the new phone finally buzzed to life, she called him immediately. He answered with a roar, accusing her of cheating with Jerry, a man she hadn't even spoken to since the carnival. When she dared to ask Jeff to help pay for the thousand-dollar device he had just snapped, he spat back,

"That's your fault for having pics of you and Jerry. Go fuck Jerry like you were in your pics." He was belligerent, cruel, and entirely convinced of his own righteousness.

Sasha spent the rest of the night in a defensive crouch, eventually turning the phone off to escape the barrage of demeaning texts. But by the next morning, the silk sheet returned. Instead of demanding payment for property damage or an apology for his terrifying behavior, Sasha found herself standing before him, begging for forgiveness.

She apologized for the photo's existence. She apologized for the cloud storage. She apologized for having a life before him. Even as Jeff realized the photos were not recent, even as the cheating accusation fell apart, he refused to back down. He simply pivoted, telling her she was wrong for keeping it, for not scrubbing her history clean for him. Exhausted and desperate to stop the bleeding of the relationship, Sasha accepted the blame. She stood there in the light of a new day, apologizing to the man who broke her phone for the sin of having a memory.

Jeff's demands came with a cold, uncompromising finality. He didn't just want the photos of Jerry gone; he wanted Sasha's entire digital existence burned to the ground.

"Delete the Facebook profile," he commanded. "Make a new one if you must, with no Jerry, no old friends. Just a clean slate." Jeff demanded.

Sasha agreed, but she was going to tag him as her boyfriend on the new profile. He declined instantly, telling her he felt social media was perverted and impersonal. It was a classic Jeff maneuver, framing his desire to remain single online as a sign of his deep, private soul. He never apologized for the phone. He never apologized for anything. Instead, he weaponized his alleged mental fragility, acting as though his broken psyche was a debt Sasha was obligated to pay. He gaslit her until the truth was unrecognizable, making her feel that every boundary she tried to set was actually a direct attack on him.

Sasha gave in. She sat down in the silence and began the systematic deletion of her life. She nuked her Facebook and cleared her cloud storage, watching years of memories vanish into a digital white void. In her haste to appease him, she even lost photos of the two of them from early in their relationship, the smiles at the bar and his backyard before the storm. When she told him, Jeff didn't care. In fact, he seemed relieved. He didn't want a record. He didn't want to be captured. He wanted to exist entirely in the shadows where he could redefine reality whenever he pleased. He stayed one step ahead of the law, knowing exactly how to keep Sasha understanding and apologetic so she would never report him for the thousands of dollars' worth of property he had destroyed.

After days of intense, suffocating closeness, a period where he made her feel like she was the only person who truly understood his darkness, Jeff delivered the final blow.

"Move in with me," he said, his voice soft, dropping that vulnerable register. "It would be easier. We'd be together. No more driving back and forth."

Sasha, exhausted from the fighting and the digital isolation, felt a strange, twisted sense of honor wash over her. She felt chosen. She felt like she had finally won the grueling game of his affection by proving she was willing to sacrifice everything, her friends, her history, and her dignity just to occupy his space.

"Yes," She whispered.

She smiled, completely oblivious to the fact that she wasn't moving into a home; she was willingly stepping into the very center of the web she had spent months helping him weave.

CHAPTER 8: *A Honeymoon in the Smoke*

For a few weeks, the house hummed with a deceptive harmony. It was spotless. With Sasha there, the frat house filth evaporated under the scent of lemon polish and fresh laundry. Even Jeff seemed transformed; he slid dishes into the dishwasher with a domestic ease that made Sasha feel like she was the missing link he had been searching for. She told herself she was the one who had finally completed him, the woman who had mended his broken chain of life. She watched him move through the clean kitchen and felt a surge of pride, convinced that her love had finally stabilized the chaos of the blue-eyed man.

But the beauty was only skin-deep. Total control wasn't enough for Jeff; he needed a level of devotion that didn't exist in the human heart. Behind the clean floors, his sweet demeanor became a mask he wore only when he wanted something. He sat in the perfectly clean living room, staring at her with eyes that had gone completely cold again. Sasha had given him everything, her life, her history, and her digital freedom, and yet, as she looked at him, she realized that in Jeff's world, *everything* was just the starting price, and he was already looking for a way to raise the cost.

Late August bled into a sweltering September, and the domestic facade settled into a repetitive, chemical rhythm. They partied together, the lines of coke cutting through the humid nights while Jeff maintained a steady, daily baseline of alcohol. Sasha joined him, echoing his pace. Whenever he grew shifty or agitated, she retreated into a strategic silence, chalking his jagged moods up to the bipolar label Syrena had handed her. She treated his temper like a storm she could simply wait out, never realizing she was standing in the eye of a hurricane.

~~~

The night started with the usual fun. When Jeff suggested calling her connection, Sasha didn't hesitate. To prove she had nothing to hide, she made
~~~

the call right in front of him, keeping her voice casual. But as the line rang, Jeff leaned in, his eyes bright with a hungry, predatory light.

"Ask him if he has any hard," he whispered.

Sasha frowned, the word unfamiliar.

"What?" she asked.

But the dealer had already heard. Through the speaker, the voice was flat:

“Yeah. How much?”

When she hung up, the confusion lingered.

"What was that about?" she asked.

Jeff's swagger was back, a dark, electric energy radiating off him.

"Let’s go," he said, grabbing his keys. "I like hard better than coke."

Despite the memory of the glass pipe hidden on the high TV stand, Sasha let herself be led. She didn't want to ruin his excitement; she wanted to be the woman who gave him exactly what he craved.

At the house they now shared, the hard was revealed. Sasha watched as he broke out the pipe. The sizzle was so familiar to him; he appeared so comforted by the sound as it filled the room. He inhaled as the rocks in the pipe began to dance. She sat nearby, pouring her powder onto a plate, but her eyes were locked on him. He looked hypnotic, glassy-eyed, flushed, and radiating a raw, carnal heat that made her breath hitch. He looked so sexy in his high that she didn't just want him; she wanted to feel what he felt. She wanted to bridge the final gap between them.

She didn't need to be forced. She saw his swagger, his distorted gentleness, and she wanted the man she saw in that reflection; she wanted to feel what he felt, she wanted to be him right there. She smoothly slid the pipe from his hand and held it to her lips.

"Okay, do whatever to make this work, I wanna try it". She said as she stroked his leg with her other hand.

The night dissolved into a fever dream of skin and adrenaline. They played gin rummy for hours, between sharing the pipe, stripped bare and fueled by a chemical intensity that made every card feel like a revelation. The sex that followed was unlike anything she had ever experienced a marathon of friction and focus that lasted for hours. In her distorted state, his inability to ejaculate wasn't a side effect; it was a gift. It was a testament to his stamina, to his desire, to the connection she thought they were finally forging.

The next day, the sun stayed behind the blinds. They spent the morning entangled in the sheets, drifting between sleep and sex, again and again. To Sasha, it felt like they had finally reached the peak of intimacy. She felt special, vital; she was no longer just his driver or his clerk. She was his connection to the high he had been longing for. She didn't realize that the connection she felt wasn't to Jeff, but to the drug he was using to replace her. She was the one providing the score, and in the twisted logic of the house, that made her the most important person in the world until the bag went empty, and the pipe burned out.

The honeymoon of the high evaporated into a cold, jagged morning-after. As soon as the rush faded, Jeff would descend into a pit of intense self-loathing. He scavenges the house, grabbing the hidden pipes and lighters and hurling them into the trash with a theatrical disgust.

Sasha realized that as long as he smoked alone, he could lie to himself. But now that she was partaking, now that he had to look at her glassy eyes, he could no longer deny the rot. To punish her for witnessing his truth, he grew even colder.

~~~

Sasha began to treat her small stash of coke like a precious secret, hiding it in a safe he couldn't reach, knowing that if he found it, he wouldn't share a hot night with her; he would simply cook it down into crack and disappear into the smoke alone, the way he preferred it.

~~~

Autumn arrived in rural New York, painting the trees in brilliant, deceptive colors. Business was booming; the new commercial facility contract Jeff landed brought in a flood of cash that should have made them happy. But as the work slowed down, the hunger returned. Jeff didn't want a partner anymore; he wanted the isolation of his vice.

One night, fueled by a drunken stupor, Jeff's swagger turned into a physical assault. In the dark of the bed they shared, Jeff began to kick her, violently. He didn't just push her; he drove his feet into her ribs, his voice a low, rhythmic hiss of insults and names. Sasha scrambled out of the bed, her heart hammering against her chest, and spent the rest of the night curled into a shivering ball in the far corner of the couch while he continued to spew venom at her from the darkness of his bedroom.

The next morning, Jeff woke up with the blank stare of an addict's amnesia. He looked at the empty side of the bed, became angry, and found Sasha shivering on the couch.

"Why weren't you in bed?" he demanded, the accusation already forming. "Where did you go? Who the fuck were you texting? You're cheating on me, aren't you?" Jeff accused.

He had absolutely no memory of the kicks or the screams. He only knew that she had escaped his physical grip, and in his mind, that choice was a betrayal.

Sasha had reached her limit. She saw the crack for what it was, the third person in their relationship, the one who stole his memory and replaced it with pure malice. She vowed never to touch the pipe again. She made the call. She rented the moving truck. She contacted Jackie, a friend who was ready to be her absolute lifeline, and began packing the few belongings she had left.

She sat at the kitchen island, her bags packed tight, waiting for Jackie to arrive. Jeff emerged from the shower, steam clinging to his skin, looking like the clear-eyed man she had first met at the bar. He looked at her, his expression bright, as if the midnight bruises on her ribs didn't even exist.

"Hey," he said casually, rubbing a towel over his hair, with his usual arrogance. "You want to go shopping for snowmobiles with me today?"

The psychological whiplash was staggering. He wasn't apologizing because, to him, there was nothing to apologize for. He was offering a new investment, a new fun distraction to bury the trauma of the night before. Sasha looked at the phone, then up at him. The lure of the good Jeff, the one who wanted to take her shopping and plan a winter of fun, was a siren song.

Sasha picked up the phone and called Jackie.

"Return the rental," She whispered through the receiver. “He wants to work it out,”

The fury on the other end of the line was a physical force. Jackie had arranged the truck and was looking out for her safety, only to be discarded in favor of the vague promise of a snowmobile. Jackie knew what Sasha didn't want to admit: this wasn't a fresh start. It was just a new season in the exact same cage.

Sasha hung up the phone, the bridge to her friend burning to ash behind her, and looked back at Jeff. She was staying for the man who kicked her, desperately hoping that a snowmobile and a clean house would finally be enough to appease him and keep the *hard* away.

CHAPTER 9: *Lie in the Bed You made*

The promise of the snowmobile evaporated as quickly as the steam from Jeff's shower.

They took the drive, they looked at the gleaming fourteen-thousand-dollar machines, but the reality of their finances, gutted by the hard and the liquor, was a cold bucket of water. Jeff didn't want a basic model; his pride demanded every add-on, every luxury, pushing the price into the realm of fantasy. In the end, all Sasha got was a helmet. It sat in the back of the Honda, a plastic trophy of a life they would never actually lead. The old snowmobile remained in the yard, a rusted, barely running skeleton that Jeff never bothered to fix.

A few nights later, the domestic peace felt genuine. They had spent the day working side by side, drywalling and painting, the physical labor creating a sense of shared purpose. As Jeff stood at the stove cooking dinner, Sasha leaned against the island, looking at their handiwork with a sense of pride.

"We should take some photos of the improvements," she said nonchalantly, her mind purely on his future. "If you ever decide to sell, these photos will prove the value. You'll get a much better price."

She meant it as a gift, a smart woman looking out for her man's investment. But the word *"sell" acted as* a trigger. In a heartbeat, the adorable man at the stove vanished. Jeff's face contorted, his features twisting into something unrecognizable. It was a transformation so sudden and so dark that Sasha felt a chill of genuine terror; it didn't look like anger, it looked like possession.

Without a word, Jeff grabbed the frying pan from the burner. With one violent, sweeping motion, he flung the shimmering, hot oil across the kitchen island directly toward Sasha's face. She ducked by pure survival instinct, the searing liquid missing her head by an inch and splattering against the freshly repaired wall behind her.

"Why did you do that?" she screamed, her heart hammering against her ribs.

Jeff stood over the stove, his eyes flat and demonic. "You don't get to tell me what I am going to do with my house!" he roared.

The rage was disproportionate, a jagged, terrifying explosion of territorial dominance. He didn't care about the profit; he only cared that she had dared to imply any influence over his domain.

He didn't stop with the oil. He surged toward her, his voice a relentless, booming wall of noise that chased her all the way to the front door. He lunged at her, his physical presence forcing her out into the cold night air. Before she could grab her keys, her wallet, or her new phone, the heavy thud of the door echoed through the yard.

The click of the deadbolt was final.

Sasha stood in the driveway, the sharp autumn air biting through her thin shirt. She tried the Honda's handle; it was unlocked, but without her keys, the ignition remained dark. She had no way to leave and nowhere to go. Defeated, she crawled into the backseat of the car, curling into a ball as the lights in the house went out one by one. She slept in the pitch black, just feet away from the man who had almost blinded her, realizing that the empty snowmobile helmet in the back was the only protection she had left in a world that had become entirely unsafe.

The next morning, she waited, her eyes fixed on the front door, hoping for a repentant lover. Instead, she got a landlord.

When the door finally creaked open, Jeff didn't look at her. He didn't ask if she was frozen or hungry. He simply reached out and heaved her purse, containing her keys, her phone, and her identity, onto the gravel. He treated her life like a bag of kitchen scraps.

Sasha got out of the car and collected her bag. She tried the front door knob and her key, but the door wouldn't budge. He had barricaded himself inside, a heavy chair wedged tight against the handle, physically sealing her out of the home she had cleaned and decorated.

"I assume you want to be alone, Jeff!" she yelled, her voice cracking in the autumn air. She even threw him a lifeline of care.

"Well, at least he seems alive," she said, hoping he'd hear her concern and feel a pang of guilt.

He didn't. The house remained as silent as a tomb.

With nowhere else to go, Sasha turned to the only person who never judged a disaster: Syrena. Syrena was always home, drifting through the days on disability and the fog of her own traumas. For Syrena, Sasha's arrival was a windfall; she got to bask in the presence of the woman she was infatuated with, and Sasha, desperate for a distraction, was happy to foot the bill.

They followed the familiar, destructive script. A box of cheap wine, a bottle of vodka, and a gram of coke. They spent the day snorting their blues away, the chemicals numbing the memory of the flying hot oil and the cold car. Syrena, caught in her own cycle of poorly-healed surgeries and bipolar swings, didn't offer any real advice. She was a yes-man in the truest sense. She didn't need to tell Sasha to leave; she just needed Sasha to stay high enough to remain in the room.

As the high leveled out, Sasha's brilliant mind began looking for a way back into Jeff's world. She noticed she was missing her jewelry, the small, gold pieces of herself she'd left behind in the chaos. It was the perfect excuse. She didn't text him about the oil or the lockout; she texted about the drywall bucket he used as a nightstand.

SASHA: Is my jewelry sitting on the drywall bucket beside the bed?

JEFF: Yeah. He replied.

That one word was the crack in the door. It wasn't an apology, and it wasn't a reconciliation, but in the warped logic of their relationship, it was communication. To Sasha, *yeah* meant he was talking. It meant he hadn't replaced her yet. It meant the "silk sheet" could be laid down once again.

She pulled the Honda into the familiar driveway, her heart thudding against her ribs. She approached the porch with the caution of someone entering a cage with a sleeping predator.

When she reached for the knob, she half expected the cold resistance of the deadbolt or the weight of the chair.

Instead, it turned.

The door was unlocked. A wave of pathetic relief washed over her. She knew him well enough to know what that meant: the moment she had reached out about the jewelry, he had signaled his move. He had removed the barricade, not because he was sorry, but because he was ready to be served again. He had waited for her to come crawling back, and she had arrived right on schedule.

The house was quiet, the air inside still smelling faintly of the cooking oil he had flung the night before. The plants she had hung so carefully were starting to droop, a silent testament to the twenty-four hours of neglect. Sasha moved through the shadows of the living room toward the bedroom, her eyes landing on the drywall-bucket nightstand where her jewelry sat, a small, golden pile of bait.

She didn't grab the rings and leave. She stood there, looking at the rumpled bed, waiting for the adorable version of the man to wake up and replace the demon from the kitchen. She was willing to overlook the oil, the lockout, and the cold car just for a moment of the intensity he offered. She was back in the cycle, convinced that the healing she was about to receive was worth the physical and emotional scars she was collecting.

Sasha didn't ask for an apology, and Jeff didn't offer one. Instead, she fell back into the role that made her feel safe: the fixer. She looked at the twisted, messy sheets, a physical representation of their shattered peace.

"Get off, I will make the bed," she said, her voice sounding hollow even to her own ears. "I sure can't sleep in this disaster."

Jeff obeyed without a word, his body moving with a sluggish, ghost-like quality. He wandered into the kitchen, the familiar clinking of ice against glass signaling the start of the nightly ritual. The disaster of the bed was easy to fix; the disaster of the oil on the wall and the bruises on her heart were not.

"You pick up any vodka?" his voice drifted in from the kitchen.

"You didn't ask me to," Sasha replied.

It was a redundant exchange. She knew he was out. They lived their lives in one-seven-five-liter increments. A massive handle of vodka every twenty-four hours was their baseline. When they were together, they shared the burden of the bottle; when they were apart, he carried it alone. It was the only thing in their lives that remained consistent.

As Sasha snapped the sheets tight, smoothing out the wrinkles, her mind began to spiral. The brilliant part of her tried to analyze the wreckage. *How do we fix this?* she wondered. *Were we ever actually good, or was the "good" just a high we were chasing?*

She thought back to the bar, and the way his blue eyes used to look when they were full of fire instead of static. She realized with a sickening jolt that their best moments were always tied to a substance: coke, vodka, or crack. Their love wasn't a foundation; it was a symptom.

Jeff returned to the bedroom, handing her a mixed drink like a peace offering that cost him nothing. It was the sexual healing prelude, the liquid courage required to pretend the previous night hadn't happened.

"I'm running to the liquor store before they close," he muttered.

He didn't ask if she wanted to go or needed anything, nor did he ask if she was okay after sleeping in the car. He just moved toward the door, already focused on the next bottle. Sasha sat on the freshly made bed, the cold glass in her hand, realizing that the cycle wasn't just vicious, it was a closed loop. She had made the bed, and now, quite literally, she had to lie in it.

CHAPTER 10: *Sinking Ships and Backhands*

The domestic routine settled into a heavy, suffocating rhythm. Sasha embraced the role of the good servant, finding a strange, numbing peace in the chores and the silence. The house stayed clean, the invoices were managed, and the outside world ceased to exist. They were two ghosts haunting a tiny house, tethered together by a shared history of violence and a mutual need for the high.

The only place where the toxicity felt like passion was the bedroom. It was their sanctuary and their ritual. They were great at it, a physical compatibility that acted as a powerful adhesive for the relationship. They watched porn together, lost in a world of curated desire, and spent hours in an endless cycle of massage and intimacy. For Sasha, this was the healing she had been chasing. In the dark, under the weight of his body or the touch of his hands, she could pretend the hot oil and the midnight kicks were just a bad dream. He was present, he was focused entirely on her, and for those few hours, the demon stayed in the shadows.

But the hard always came back. It wasn't a romantic choice anymore; it was a structural necessity. Jeff needed the fix, and Sasha was now a permanent fixture in his life. He didn't necessarily want her to partake, and she didn't necessarily want to smoke, but the drug had become the third member of their household.

Jeff's need for her was visceral, but it wasn't love; it was utility. Without her, he had no one to act as his emotional lightning rod. He had no punching bag to blame for his failures and no one to degrade with his favorite insults. He told her, with a chilling lack of shame, about the old ways he'd have to return to if she left: the dating apps, the frantic scrolling, the occasional call to a prostitute. He used his past transgressions as a threat, making her feel like she was the only thing standing between him and total depravity.

Sasha felt a dark sense of purpose in being the one he needed. She convinced herself that her presence was a stabilizing force, even as she watched him crumble. She stayed because the chaos had become her comfort zone. The unpredictability of his moods, the intensity of the makeup sex, and the shared crack use created a world that was far more exciting than the boring life she had with Jerry or her ex-husband James.

She looked at her hanging plants now thriving in the humid, smoke-filled air and realized they were like her: adapted to a hostile environment. They had both found a way to grow in the dark. She didn't want to leave because, for the first time in her life, she felt entirely indispensable. She was the witness, the dealer, the maid, and the lover. She was the one who kept the demon at bay, unaware that by staying, she was only feeding it.

The atmosphere in the bar was already thick with the familiar smell of stale beer and the electric hum of the first-line rush. Sasha felt comfortable here; she was in her element, driving the Honda, holding the stash, and standing beside a man who looked like the king of the room. But that comfort was shattered the moment Tom approached them.

Tom didn't lead with a *hello*. He led with a grenade. As an employee of Jeff's brother, John, he had the front-row seat to the family feud.

"John's telling everyone he fired you because you were smoking crack and no-showing," Tom said, his eyes darting between Jeff and Sasha.

Whether Tom was looking for a blowout or genuinely trying to warn them didn't matter. The damage was done.

Sasha felt the air leave her lungs. She looked at Jeff and saw her adorable partner vanish, replaced instantly by the demon. His eyes turned a jagged, predatory blue. The irony was suffocating: John was telling the absolute truth, and they both knew it. The crack, the missed shifts, the spiral, it was all real. To Jeff, the insulting truth was the ultimate insult.

Jeff didn't crumble under the weight of the accusation. Instead, he pivoted. His reputation was a holy thing to him, even as he systematically lit it on fire. He couldn't beat his brother's employee in the middle of the bar, so he decided to murder his brother's character instead.

"You want the truth?" Jeff projected his voice just loud enough for the surrounding tables to hear, his swagger morphing into a calculated performance of the betrayed savior.

He spun a frantic, elaborate lie. He claimed John was the one spiraling, a cocaine addict who was running the family business into the ground. Jeff claimed he was the hero who had stepped in to save the company, and that John had fired him simply to avoid paying back the thousands Jeff had invested to keep the business afloat.

"Yeah, I had a crack problem years ago," Jeff admitted with a practiced, humble shrug, "but I went to rehab. I sweated it out in my mother's basement. I've been clean since I was twenty-four." Jeff demanded.

It was a brilliant performance. By admitting a past mistake, he made his current lies feel like hard-won truths. Sasha stood beside him, playing the role of the supportive partner, nodding along to a story she knew was a total fabrication. She watched him defend his honor, while her own purse was heavy with the very drugs his brother had accused him of using.

They stayed at the bar, fueled by the adrenaline of the lie. Despite the rehab story Jeff had just broadcast to the room, the two of them began a frantic rotation to the bathrooms, swapping the bag between them. Every fifteen minutes, they took turns slipping away to do another line, emerging with jaw clenches and sniffles they thought were invisible to the other patrons.

They stood in the center of the room, convinced they were the smartest people in the building. Jeff was high on his own reinvented history, and Sasha was high on the coke and the thrill of being his ride-or-die. They didn't see the regulars whispering or the bartender's knowing glances. They were two people standing on a sinking ship, convinced they were the ones who owned the ocean.

Sasha leaned against the bar, laughing with a familiar waitress, her world narrowed down to the bright, sharp clarity of the high. She felt untouchable. She watched the two unfamiliar girls drift toward the bathroom, and in her mind, she was still the queen of the room. She didn't notice, or perhaps she chose not to see Jeff peeling away from the crowd.

Jeff was in full ladies' man mode, his ego fed by the newcomers' fresh eyes. He didn't just want to talk; he wanted to show off the power he thought he had. He wanted to be the guy with the stash and the keys to the castle.

He led one of the new girls toward the back, his swagger leading him right into the bar owner's open private office. It was a bold, reckless move. He laid out the lines on the mahogany desk, treating the space like it was his own personal VIP lounge.

But Tom was watching. Tom trailed them like a shark, then leaned over the bar and whispered in the bartender's ear.

The explosion was instantaneous. The bartender, terrified for his liquor license and his job, didn't play it cool. He burst into the office, his voice a serrated blade.

"Get the fuck out! Now! Or I'm calling the cops!"

Jeff didn't go quietly. Being caught red-handed triggered a white-hot righteous fury. He lunged at the bartender, his voice booming through the small office and into the main bar area.

"You don't talk to me like that!" he roared, his eyes snapping to Tom, who was standing in the doorway with a smirk that gave him away.

Jeff's brain, fueled by the coke and the demon within, immediately locked onto Tom as the culprit.

In the main barroom, the music seemed to dip as the shouting started. Sasha stood by the waitress, her drink halfway to her lips, her heart dropping into her stomach. She heard Jeff's voice, that specific, jagged roar that had previously preceded a broken phone or a puddle of hot oil. She had no idea what had happened in the back room, but she knew the perfect evening was over. The ladies' man had been outed as a common trespasser, and as the bartender threatened to call the police, Sasha realized that her Honda was about to become their getaway car once again.

Sasha surged toward the office, her voice a frantic plea for him to stop. But when Jeff turned to look at her, his eyes were cold and accusatory, a silent accusation that, somehow, her presence was the cause of his downfall.

Driven by the need to reclaim his dominance, Jeff swung at Tom with every ounce of his cocaine-fueled rage. But his coordination was completely shot. He missed Tom's face by a foot, the momentum of his own hate carrying him forward until he slammed face-first into the dirty floor.

The sound that followed was worse than a punch: it was a snicker. The girl Jeff had been trying to impress didn't look horrified; she looked amused. She, like every other regular in the room, saw him for exactly what he was: a boastful, spiraling addict. Only Sasha still held onto the myth of his greatness.

The owner's verdict came down like a gavel. Despite the work Jeff had done on the rooftop units, despite his history as a regular, he was banned.

Sasha knelt beside him, reaching out to help him up, a reflex of the servant she had become. But Jeff slapped her hand away, his face contorting into an evil stare that promised retribution. He managed to scramble to his feet, the embarrassment radiating off him like heat.

They retreated to the Honda. Sasha sat behind the wheel, her hands trembling, her mind racing for a way to fix the atmosphere. She stayed quiet, waiting for the storm to pass. In a desperate attempt to soothe the beast, she offered the only peace pipe she knew:

"Do you want me to get you some hard?" She asked as she drove cautiously down the road.

The backhand came out of nowhere. It was a fast, heavy strike that connected with the side of her head, snapping her neck to the side.

The world went completely silent. The sound of the engine, the wind against the windshield, it all vanished, replaced by a high-pitched, piercing ring that vibrated in her skull. Her ear went dead, the physical shock of the blow echoing through her entire body.

Sasha stared at the road ahead, her vision swimming, trying to process the fact that the man she had just defended had physically marked her. Beside her, Jeff didn't look sorry. He sat there with a shit-eating grin, his posture relaxed, his eyes satisfied. In his twisted mind, the hierarchy had been restored. He might have lost the bar, he might have fallen on the floor, but he still had his punching bag.

Sasha didn't have the strength to sleep in the Honda again. She walked into the house, a ghost in her own life, and placed the remaining bags of coke on the counter, a final tribute to a man who had just deafened her. She retreated to the bedroom, closing the door on the sound of Jeff's frantic, chemical energy.

Through the thin walls, she heard the rhythm of his night. The bathroom door opening and closing, the pacing in the kitchen, the low light of his phone screen reflecting off the hallway walls. He wasn't mourning their relationship or feeling the weight of his hands on her face; he was back in the digital hunt, scrolling through the old familiar ways to find a fresh supply of attention.

The next morning, the mirror told a story Sasha wasn't ready to read. Her lip was swollen, a dark, bruised handprint blossoming across her cheek like a brand. When Jeff emerged, she didn't meet him with a suitcase or a police report. She met him with a joke.

"I never realized why they call it getting your bell rung until last night," she said, letting out a shaky, desperate laugh while he stood at the stove.

Jeff didn't flinch. He didn't apologize. Instead, he joined her in the laughter. He looked at her and saw a perfect instrument that he could play however he liked, knowing she would always stay in tune with his demands.

As the drugs began to leave their systems, the crash brought with it a hollow, desperate need for connection. Jeff began the make-up ritual with a calculated, predatory softness. He moved behind her, his hands, the same hands that had silenced her ear, now tracing the curves of her body. He pressed against her, the heat of his skin acting like a sedative for her trauma.

They fell into bed and stayed there for hours, lost in a marathon of sex that felt like a sanctuary. To Sasha, the intensity of his touch felt like love, a sexual healing that wiped away the memory of the bar and the backhand. She leaned into the sensation, completely unaware that he had just set the final seal on the cage. He had hit her, he had humiliated her, and now he was rewarding her for staying. As they lay together in the quiet of the afternoon, Sasha felt connected, while Jeff simply felt satisfied that the fiddle was back in its case.

CHAPTER 11: *Clarity in the Crossfire*

Jeff's phone buzzed on the arm of the couch while Sasha doted on him, massaging his feet. He looked at the screen and abruptly pulled his hands away from hers.

"My mother," he said, clearing his throat, "She needs to talk to me about something."

His voice carried its usual arrogance. It was clear that in his wildest thoughts, Jeff didn't believe his family had heard a single rumor about what had happened at the tavern. His mind couldn't fathom that anyone would see his carefully curated facade as anything less than perfect.

The drive to his mother's camp was filled with Jeff's typical bravado He rolled along with the entitled attitude of royalty, and Sasha kept her peace, letting him emit that familiar, protective strength. When they arrived at the camp, the scenery was bountiful: the trees, the mountains, and the deep lake were breathtaking, but the atmosphere waiting for them inside was a trap neither of them had prepared for.

Sitting across the dinner table from Tara, John's wife meant facing a direct line to the brother he had tried to defame. When Tara began to press him about the bar incident, Jeff's standard defense was to bark, dismiss, and shut the conversation down. But his mother wasn't playing the role of the silent victim.

The silence that followed his mother's accusation was heavy and suffocating. Sasha, caught in the crossfire, could only sip her drink, cataloging every word as a chilling confirmation of her darkest fears.

Jeff's mother didn't just scold him; she systematically dismantled his entire life story. She knew about the dope. She knew about the history. She saw straight through the frantic lies he had spun to the town about John.

Then came the ultimate blow: the inheritance. It was a final, tangible consequence for his behavior. His mother flatly refused Jeff any access to her cabin, leaving it all to John upon her passing. As she framed it, he disrespected family first and second; John would take care of it, whereas Jeff would not. For Jeff, being cut off publicly like this wasn't just about the loss of his childhood cabin; it was the ultimate humiliation. A formal acknowledgment from his own blood that he had failed.

Before the night ended, Jeff's mother looked directly at Sasha.

"Honey, you'd better know my son has lots of monsters inside his head."

The warning hung in the air, cold and definitive. It was a rare moment of absolute clarity from someone who had watched the cycle play out for decades. She wasn't just talking about a substance; she was talking about a fundamental brokenness that no amount of cleaning, fixing, or affection could ever mend.

For the first time since Sasha had known him, Jeff didn't explode. He didn't throw anything or snap a phone. The physical presence of his mother and Tara created a boundary he couldn't push past. Outnumbered and outgunned, he chose a tactical retreat.

He muttered to Sasha to take the booze up to the spare room. They had planned to stay the night because it was a long drive, and now he desperately needed to escape the room. It was a rare moment of restraint, born of absolute defeat rather than growth.

The drive back after daybreak was a silent, grim affair. The Honda felt smaller and more restrictive than ever as they wound through the mountain roads. Sasha, mourning the disastrous introduction to his family, was forced to sit with the reality that Jeff's demons weren't a secret she could help him hide. They were a documented, permanent family legacy.

Upon their return, the house they shared felt entirely different. The toxic perfection was replaced by a heavy, contemplative silence. Jeff sat on the couch, staring into space, brooding over the wreckage of his reputation. But for a man like Jeff, that kind of brooding rarely led to self-reflection; it usually just deepened the bitter resentment toward the world that had exposed him. Sasha moved through the quiet kitchen, looking at her thriving plants, left to wonder about the gravity of the trip. If his own mother had completely given up on him, what was she still doing there? She had felt his violence, heard the warnings, and witnessed the loss of his legacy. Yet she was still the one carrying the bottle into the room.

CHAPTER 12: *Karma is a Beach*

The violence evolved. It was no longer an explosive, hot-oil rage; it became a cold, rhythmic intimidation. Jeff took to drinking himself into a dark depression, and while Sasha pretends to sleep, he vents his frustration on the architecture of their lives. The heavy thud of his fist hitting the bedroom drywall, inches from where her head lay, was a deliberate message.

Sasha became a very light sleeper; her body physically tuned to the sound of his breathing and the shifting of his weight. She played dead, keeping her eyes shut and her breathing steady, realizing that to acknowledge his anger is to invite it onto herself. She was a prisoner of the house, even when he was only whispering his malice to the walls.

The brooding Jeff did after the trip to his mother's cabin didn't lead to a breakthrough; it led to a total breakdown. He spends days in a state of inconsolable weeping. But the tears weren't for the mother he had alienated, the woman whose life he had derailed, nor for his brother's reputation that he had attempted to slaughter. He cries entirely for himself. He mourned the ladies' man from the tavern, the successful businessman his brother fired, and the good son his mother had disinherited.

He blamed Sasha for the vacuum in his life. In his twisted logic, if she were better, smarter, or more obedient, he wouldn't feel this way. He used her as a repository for his failures. When he wasn't blaming her, he ignored her, lost in a heavy fog where his ego is the only thing that mattered.

They were barely holding it together, a phrase that implied a shared effort, but the reality was that Sasha was the only one gripping the rope. She carried her own bottled-up sadness like a physical weight. The manic toxic perfection was gone, replaced by a grim, exhausting endurance.

The arguments were no longer about big things, the drugs or the cheating, but about the minutiae of their miserable coexistence. Every sigh, every look, every clink of a glass was a potential trigger. They existed in a state of mutual, silent rot.

As the anniversary of their meeting at the bar approaches, Sasha looks around the tiny house. The plants she hung were struggling in the dim winter light, much like her. She has stayed for the passion, she has stayed for the healing, and now she is staying for the depression. She was still his driver, his clerk, and his silent witness, but the early days felt like a lifetime ago. She was no longer waiting for him to come back to her; she was just waiting for the next blow to fall, whether it was against the wall or against her skin.

Then, Jeff proposed a trip to visit his father and stepmother in Florida. He has a deep-seated need to make something right among his family, to soothe his bruised pride, and the perfect targets were the people who had the least amount of contact with his daily reality. His father and stepmother adored him; she found him even more gorgeous than a TV actor. If Jeff could woo anyone, it was the father who had split from his mother when Jeff was only nine years old to marry a neighbor. He had left his boys to be raised entirely by their mother, but from thousands of miles away, he still held his son in high regard.

The shift from the gray, stagnant atmosphere of New York to the blinding neon and palm trees of Florida represents a desperate Hail Mary. For Jeff, this wasn't a vacation; it was a stage. He is moving from a theater where everyone knows his demons to one where he can rewrite the script entirely.

As the plane touched down, the weight of the previous year seemed to lift, if only superficially. The bright, unrelenting Florida sun acted as a bleach, momentarily whitening the stains of the hot-oil incident, the dead ear, and the midnight wall-punching. Jeff played the part of the successful, loving partner with a veteran's skill. Away from the townies and the brother who had outed him, he could breathe again; he could redeem himself in the eyes of his father, who relished Jeff's ongoing friction with his mother.

For Sasha, the optimism felt like a survival instinct. She was exhausted from a year of hyper-vigilance and bottled-up sadness. The idea of meeting Jeff's father and stepmother offered a glimmer of hope: maybe, in their eyes, he was still the golden boy. If she could just win them over, maybe she could finally find a stable foundation for the situationship she was trapped in.

Jeff's father and stepmother were his final stronghold of ignorance. They sided with Jeff, not because he was right, but because he was a master of the victim narrative. To them, John and Tara were the agitators, and Jeff was the misunderstood, hardworking son. They were entirely clueless about the crack, the vodka handles, and the fact that Jeff's business was a slow-motion train wreck. Jeff wasn't bringing Sasha to Florida to introduce her to his family; he was bringing her as a beautiful prop to prove that his life was perfect.

The reality beneath the tan was grimmer. The business had slowed to a crawl, and the money for luxury was nonexistent. They were lying low because they had to, not because they wanted to. The depression that had anchored Jeff to the bedroom floor for months was still there, masked by the glare of the sun.

Sasha sat in the rental car, looking at the passing palm trees and feeling the knot of nerves in her stomach. She knew, deep down, that a change of scenery didn't change a soul. The opulent marble and manicured lawns of the Florida estate served as the ultimate backdrop for Jeff's greatest performance. In this house of wealth and order, he wasn't an addict; he was the prodigal son, returning in triumph with a brilliant woman on his arm.

Sasha moved through the majestic home as if she were walking through a museum of the life she felt she deserved. Looking at the pristine surfaces and the high-end décor, she couldn't help but wonder why Jeff, the man with the commanding, deep voice and the incredible presence, couldn't maintain this level of order back home.

Jeff was at his most dangerous here because he was at his most charming.

With his dark, sensual hair peeking out from his hat and his tone assertive yet soft, he radiated a confidence that made his father's skepticism melt away. When the inevitable question about John and the drug rumors came up, Jeff executed a total character assassination. He painted John as a greedy, drug-addled traitor, framing himself as the victimized sibling merely trying to protect the family legacy.

Sasha sat in the heavy silence that followed, trapped by her own ride-or-die loyalty. She saw the bag of lies being sold, and she knew that to speak the truth would be to cast herself as the villain in Jeff's carefully crafted play. She stayed silent, an accomplice to the lie, bound by the luxury of the house and the fear of the man sitting next to her.

The evening ended in a guest room decorated in soft, deceptive Florida pastels, a stark contrast to the darkness about to unfold. The intimacy they sought was aggressive and pounding, a physical release of the day's performative tension. But as the adrenaline faded, the demon returned to the pillow.

In the dark of the guest room, just feet away from his father's bedroom, Jeff began to hiss. The deep, soft voice that had charmed his parents hours earlier was now a jagged weapon.

"Slut." He slurred into the dark. "You are such a whore." "I can't believe I brought you here. Slut, Sasha, you're a fucking whore, slut"

He didn't scream; he whispered the insults, letting them sink into her like calculated venom. He degraded her in the very bed his father had provided, reclaiming his dominance after a day of playing the good son. Sasha lay there, completely frozen in the pastel sheets, waiting for the barrage to end. Only when his breathing turned heavy and rhythmic did she allow herself to exhale.

The Florida sun seemed to have a bleaching effect on Jeff's psyche during the day. After the venomous whispers of the first night, he underwent another transformation. For the remainder of the week, the demon retreated, replaced by the man Sasha had fallen for at the bar, attentive, charming, and peaceful.

They spent their evenings on the Gulf Coast, watching the sky bruise into deep purples and oranges. In those moments, with the salt air between them and the New York winter a thousand miles away, it was easy to buy into the delusion of hope. Sasha let herself believe that their relationship was finally evolving.

On their last day, they surrendered completely to the vacation lifestyle. They spent the entire afternoon with their toes in the sand, indulging in platters of raw oysters and cold margaritas. It was the peak of their expensive tastes, beautiful surroundings, and a chemical buzz provided by the tequila and the sunshine.

But as the sun dipped below the horizon for the final time, the bill came due.

The flight home was scheduled for the next morning, but Jeff wouldn't be leaving with the swagger he arrived with. By late evening, the oysters or the excess caught up to him with a vengeance. He was gripped by a violent, unglamorous illness. The man who had spent the year kicking walls, throwing oil, and whispering insults into the dark was reduced to a shivering heap, trapped in the pastel-colored bathroom, anchored to the floor tile by relentless vomiting.

Sasha sat on the edge of the bed, listening to the sounds of his physical collapse echoing off the pristine walls. She didn't feel the usual surge of servant panic. She didn't rush to rub his back or offer comfort. Instead, a cold, sharp clarity settled over her.

She looked at the bathroom door, thinking of the bell he had rung in her ear and the humiliation he had forced her to swallow in front of his family. As the sounds of his misery continued, a single thought drifted through her mind with a dark, satisfying click:

Karma is a bitch.

The return to New York wasn't a crash back to reality, but rather a descent into a new, quiet kind of isolation. The food poisoning had acted as a physical purge for Jeff, stripping away his bravado and leaving him vulnerable. For a man who lived to be served, his recovery was the ultimate opportunity to test Sasha's devotion, and she had passed with flying colors.

In the days following their return, Jeff was a different man.

He was sober and grounded, and he overflowed with an affection that felt like a reward.

"You have been so good to me," he told her, his deep voice soft and seemingly sincere.

For Sasha, these words were the drug she craved more than any powder or rock. They were the validation that her servant-like heart was working, that she was finally winning the battle for his soul.

"Jeff, I love you more than anything," she replied, falling deeper into his grasp.

The bell-ringing backhand and the hot oil felt like distant memories, buried under the weight of this new, sober intimacy. She made his health her singular priority, becoming his nurse, his chef, and his shield against the world.

But this civility came at a steep price: total isolation.

Sasha's world had shrunk to the size of their tiny house. Her friends, once a vibrant part of her life, faded into the background. Even Syrena, her most loyal enabler, had stopped calling. The risk was too high; one wrong text at the wrong time could trigger the demon, and everyone knew it. Jeff had successfully pruned Sasha's life until he was the only branch left for her to cling to.

They became the Toxic Team. Banned from the local bar and disowned by his nearby family, Jeff had no supply left but Sasha. He accompanied her everywhere, to the store, to jobs, on basic errands. To an outsider, they looked like an inseparable couple; in truth, they were two people handcuffed together in a sinking boat, mistaking the stillness of the water for safety.

Sasha felt a profound sense of relief. The house was quiet. No walls were being punched, no names were being whispered in the dark, and the crack had been replaced by herbal tea and rest. She told herself that they had finally turned a corner, entirely unaware that this wasn't a new beginning. Jeff wasn't cured; he was simply refueling. His need for control hadn't vanished; it was just feasting on her undivided attention and care. In this silent, civil vacuum, Sasha was losing the last shreds of her independence, becoming so entwined with his survival that she no longer knew where she ended, and Jeff began.

CHAPTER 13: *Scars*

For months, Jeff had played the role of the recovering partner, but the crack pipe and the dating apps were never truly gone; they were just set aside, like tools in a hidden shed. Hiding it from Sasha gave him a familiar surge of superiority; the brilliant woman was being fooled by the ladies' man once again.

When morning came, and the harsh light hit the bathroom tile, the reality was pathetic: a naked, sweating man clutching a phone and a pipe. But Jeff, ever the manipulator, didn't resort to the demon rage this time. He knew he was caught, so he instantly pivoted to the Docile Jeff. He used the slurred, sexy softness of his voice to gaslight her, framing his drug use as a direct response to her going to bed. He made his betrayal her fault before the conversation could even begin.

Sasha's anger was a volatile mixture of betrayal and exhaustion. She was less afraid of the crack than she was of the phone, the digital proof that she was being replaced even while she lived in his house. But Jeff saw her anger as a challenge to his control.

The make-up ritual started with the familiar strokes on her arms, the low whispers of needing to feel her. Sasha, caught in the deep, agonizing grooves of their trauma bond, prepared for the only healing she thought they had left.

But Jeff had no intention of healing. He didn't want a partner; he wanted an object to punish for catching him in his degradation.

The assault was a total shattering of her womanhood. he forced himself in her, ignoring her screams...

"Stop, Jeff, Please!"

He was treating her body like a piece of meat to be used, broken, and discarded. In those minutes, Jeff finally dropped the mask entirely. There was no GQ poster boy left. There was only a raging lunatic who finished his business and walked away without a single word, leaving her bruised, torn, and bleeding on the couch, the same couch that she had cleaned a hundred times.

The word "*Sodomy*" whispered under her breath into the silence was the first spark of true clarity Sasha had experienced in a year. It wasn't bad sex or rough play, and it wasn't rough play; it was a violation of her existence.

The brilliant woman finally returned. She didn't wait for an apology that would never come. She didn't wait for him to wake up from his stupor and blame the dope. She grabbed the essentials, the things that defined her outside of his orbit, and she walked toward the door.

"I am done with you and this place," she yelled, her voice finally cutting through the suffocating silence of the tiny house.

With the help of her old friend, Sasha found her own sanctuary: a rental right in town, it was a ranch-style house with a single-car garage. She furnished it with pieces that were hers alone, no memories of the vacation with Jeff, no handles of vodka on the counter, and no drywall-bucket nightstands. For the first time in over a year, her environment reflected her own brilliant mind rather than Jeff's chaotic demon.

Jeff's silence was a deafening relief. Weeks passed without a single shifty text or a drunken middle-of-the-night call. Sasha knew him well enough to realize that his silence wasn't born of respect; it was born of fear. He knew exactly what he had done on that couch, and he was likely waiting for the authorities to knock on his door.

The decision not to report the assault was a heavy, complicated burden. Sasha's mind was a battlefield of logic and trauma. She knew that in a small town, a local golden boy with an assertive, deep voice and an attractive face often got the benefit of the doubt.

Then, a sickening memory resurfaced, locking the lock on her silence. Months ago, Jeff had bragged to her about an encounter, claiming he had taken a photo of her swollen, torn anatomy after a particularly rough night and passed his phone around a crowd of men at the local bar, including the owner. At the time, caught in the fog of their "toxic perfection," Sasha had felt a twisted sense of shame mixed with the belief that he was simply proud of their intense sexual connection.

Now, looking back with clear eyes, the horror of it hit her. It wasn't pride. To Jeff, her body was a trophy of his dominance to be displayed and mocked. To the townies, they were just a kinky, volatile couple who played a dangerous game.

Sasha's shame acted as a silencer. She feared that if she spoke the word *sodomy* to the local police, the small-town system would respond with a smirk, pointing to the months of aggressive *sexual healing* she had willingly participated in.

She settled into her new routine, starting fresh but living on high alert. She had seen the demon, felt the demon inside her most sacred parts, and survived. She was out of the house, but the situationship had left deep physical and psychological scars that new furniture couldn't hide.

She was safe for now, but in a small town, paths eventually cross. She had escaped the cage, but Jeff was still out there, and a narcissist with a broken ego and a crack pipe rarely stays quiet forever.

CHAPTER 14: *Concrete Roots*

Sasha knew she shouldn't, but she couldn't stop herself from sending Jeff a message about the phone bill. He hadn't sent her any money, and looking at the shared account history, she could see through the random unfamiliar numbers that he was playing his digital dating games again.

SASHA: Jeff, I need you to pay the phone bill, or get your own account.

Silence came back in return. She waited for hours, the phone heavy in her hand. Late that night, his reply finally pierced the dark.

JEFF: Meet me at the phone store, and I will get my own account. Be there at noon tomorrow.

She felt a brief surge of relief that he was finally taking responsibility for his own things, but the message's sterile tone left her cold. She was seeing his emotional detachment much more clearly now that she had her own four walls.

~~~
~~~

The meeting at the phone store, however, was a classic masterclass in narcissistic re-hooking. Jeff knew exactly how to play his hand. He used his physical beauty, his bow-legged swagger, and the deep, assertive voice that Sasha had always been powerless against. By withholding the money he owed her, he forced her into a corner where she had to negotiate, and then he offered her the one thing he knew she couldn't refuse: a sense of purpose.

While they were standing by the counter, he slouched, looking defeated, and begged for her help. He claimed he had a massive ductwork job at a commercial building, but he had no one to rely on. In reality, it wasn't about the labor; it was about reclaiming his psychological control over her under the guise of a professional partnership

"Didn't you have that Timmy kid from the bar helping you?" Sasha asked, crossing her arms.

"Sasha, he just isn't enough help," Jeff pouted, his voice dropping into that soft, manipulative register. "He has to be picked up and dropped off, and he's completely unreliable. I just need someone I can actually count on."

Sasha hesitated, the familiar pull of being his savior tugging at her.

"Fine, text me the details," Sasha said.

The commercial attic he stuck Sasha in to work became the ultimate metaphor for their entire relationship. It was hot, stifling, dark, and filled with blinding fiberglass irritants. As Sasha jumped between the wooden joists, carefully avoiding stepping through the drywall into the ceiling below, she felt an unfamiliar new sense of power.

Her secret key bumps of cocaine became her silent, invisible rebellion. Up in the dark rafters, she wasn't just his worker; she felt confident and energized, and entirely in control. What she failed to realize was that by hiding her own drug use, she was morphing into the exact creature she despised. She was becoming a person of secrets and shadows. She rationalized it by telling herself she was protecting his sobriety, but in reality, she was just lowering herself into his mud so the relationship could make sense again.

The grueling week of work finally ended, and the system was successfully installed. They both felt a rare, clean sense of shared satisfaction, and Jeff actually handed her the cash she deserved.

But the peace was fleeing. Late that Friday evening, Jeff showed up at her new pad, drunk and clutching a stolen bar glass in his hand. The old Jeff was back. His blunt, aggressive demand to fuck was a sickening reminder of the assault on his couch, but this time, Sasha found her voice. She stood her ground, using her physical space to guide his staggering, liquor-soaked body right back out the door.

For a few golden hours, she was the brilliant woman again, protected by her own locked door and her phone's *Do Not Disturb* setting, until the phone began to ring, over and over, shattering the quiet.

The local precinct number piercing through the fail-safe override of her phone was the sound of the trap snapping shut. Finding out Jeff had been arrested for his third DUI instantly vaporized the illusion of the Jeff she had worked with all week, and confirmed the booze-soaked jerk that appeared on her doorstep hours earlier.

When she picked him up from the station, and of course, she picked him up, the officer was insistent that he be released to a responsible party anywhere other than jail, a glaring byproduct of New York's bail reform.

Jeff stumbled into the passenger seat of the Honda completely unfazed and still operating in ladies' man mode, loudly claiming he had just been "busting the officer's balls." He possessed no shame, fueled entirely by the adrenaline of another narrow escape.

The pathetic truth didn't actually come out until the following afternoon. He hadn't just been driving drunk around town; he was speeding east to find his dealer.

"Cracky is gonna be so pissed at me," Jeff muttered over his food, shaking his head. "I was supposed to meet him at the gas station, damn cop caught me speeding, he was hiding out in the dark."

Sasha stared at him, disgust rising in her throat.

"You left my house to buy dope? Seriously, Jeff, when are you going to grow up?"

Jeff reached across the table, his eyes turning soft, completely rewriting history on the fly.

"Well, we both gotta clean up, Sash. We do too much of everything; we are functioning alcoholics. Let's calm down and settle down together."

He spoke as if the brutal assault on the couch never happened. He spoke as if he hadn't just tried to do it again the night before.

~~~

The *third DUI* was a life-altering catastrophe. Jeff was bound to lose his license for years, which means Sasha is now his permanent, mandatory chauffeur. By destroying his own legal right to move, he has successfully handcuffed her to his daily survival. When he muttered, "*We gotta clean up,*" it wasn't a spiritual vow of sobriety; it was
~~~

a desperate plea for her to absorb the impact of his latest explosion.

Sasha, caught in the fragile peace of the morning-after and the intoxicating thrill of being his savior yet again, accepts the pact. She demanded he be done with the crack, yet she remained silent about the baggie tucked away in her own pocket. They are now two people who have emotionally lost their licenses to live normal lives, driving together in the Honda into a bleak future defined by court dates, his dealer's potential wrath, and a shared addiction they both pretended wasn't there.

~~~

The sudden news of his mother's terminal cancer was a heavy stone for Sasha to carry, especially with the chilling warnings the woman had issued during their last meeting echoing in her mind. But Sasha, ever the compulsive fixer, pushed Jeff toward the closure she believed they both desperately needed.

The funeral, however, was nothing more than a high-stakes performance to save face. Jeff and John stood side by side in their suits, playing the part of grieving,
~~~

unified brothers for the extended family, but the air between them was as cold as ice.

When the will was read, the final, permanent blow was dealt. His mother had kept her word. While Jeff received a modest insurance payout, the historic childhood property the boys grew up at was left to John and Tara; this was a legal, permanent brand of untrustworthiness. Sasha realized then that Jeff's year-long silence toward his mother wasn't just a tiff; it was a vengeful standoff that he had ultimately, completely lost.

With his license revoked and his depression mounting, the tiny frat house became a stagnant tomb. Sasha made the executive decision: Jeff was moving into her house. She coordinated the moving truck, hired the helpers, and physically transplanted his life into her quaint, clean sanctuary. By putting his house on the market, she burned the last bridge to his geographic independence.

For the first time in their relationship, Jeff was the guest on her turf. The drastic change in scenery brought a change in behavior; the demon went dormant. Jeff completely stopped the dope and returned to being the blue-eyed man she loved, soft, dependent, and incredibly generous with his new inheritance money. He eagerly paid the bills, took care of the grocery bills, and leaned entirely on her strength.

Sasha felt an intoxicating surge of triumph. She had finally assumed the control she'd been chasing for two years. He was in her home, living on her terms, and completely reliant on her Honda to move through the world.

But this control came with a dark passenger: Jeff's depression.

He spent his days in a heavy fog of guilt and regret, mourning a mother he had disowned and a brother he had publicly slandered. Because his narcissism wouldn't allow him to admit that his own volatile actions had caused the family rift, he lived in a constant state of a shattered ego, a fragile glass structure that Sasha had to constantly piece back together.

They were tighter than they had ever been, but it was a claustrophobic tightness born of absolute isolation. There was no one else left. No Jackie, no Syrena, nobody. They fed off one another in a perfectly closed, toxic loop. Sasha felt like the boss because she held the car keys and owned the clean lease, but she was also the only structural pillar standing between Jeff and a total psychological collapse.

In her mind, she had finally saved him. In reality, she had built a beautiful, quaint cage for two. She was the warden, the nurse, and the lover, finally possessing the perfect, compliant version of Jeff, but it was a version that only existed because he had been utterly defeated by life.

CHAPTER 15: *Leave the Circus Behind*

Sasha looked at Jeff as he sat on her couch, surrounded by her furniture and breathing her air. He was quiet now, subdued by the weight of his mother's death and the mental loss of his mobility. To the outside world, she was the devoted partner saving a drowning man. But in the quiet hours of the night, as she watched him sleep, her thoughts took a more predatory turn.

She began to indulge in a vivid, recurring fantasy. In this mental theater, the situationship reached its logical, dark conclusion. She imagined him in the basement of her quaint home, not as a guest, but as a permanent fixture. She saw him tied up, physically restrained in the same way he had emotionally restrained her for years.

In her mind, this was the ultimate form of toxic perfection. She could live her life, go to the store, see her friends, do her work, and he would always be there, waiting, unable to phone a dealer, punch a wall, screw a prostitute, or scroll through a dating app. He would be her hostage: a beautiful, blue-eyed object that she could visit for sexual healing whenever she desired, entirely on her terms.

She realized with a chilling clarity that this was exactly what he had done to her for two years. He hadn't used rope or chains, but he had used her *silk sheet* weakness, her bank account, and his own demon to keep her in a state of perpetual captivity. Now, the roles were reversed. He was the one who couldn't leave. He was the one who had to wait for her to pick up the keys to the Honda if he wanted to see the sun.

There was a sick, addictive satisfaction in this new dynamic. When he was depressed and needy, she felt a surge of pure dominance. She fed him, she housed him, and she managed the money that kept them afloat. She was the one who decided when they ate, where they went, and when they were intimate.

The fantasy of the basement wasn't about pain; it was about certainty. If he was her hostage, he couldn't leave her for a slut online. He couldn't go *East* to see

Cracky. He couldn't backhand her into a world of ringing silence.

As the days passed, the line between her fantasy and their reality began to blur. Jeff was already her hostage. Every time she took his hand to lead him to the car, or every time she reminded him that he was in her house now, she was tightening the invisible knots around his wrists.

Sasha realized she didn't need the basement at all. She had something better: a man who had voluntarily surrendered his life to her because he had nowhere left to go. She watched him move through her kitchen slowly, obediently, and brokenly, and felt a dark, quiet thrill. She was no longer the good servant. She was the master of the house, and the GQ poster boy was finally exactly where she wanted him: trapped in the safety of her love.

CHAPTER 16: *The Ghost in the Rearview Mirror*

The shift happened gradually, hidden in the bottom of a bottle of red wine. Sasha found herself seduced by the luxury of the long afternoon, a slow, crimson descent into day-drinking and heavy naps. She felt empowered, thinking they were finally living the high life on his inheritance, a reward for the years of trauma she had endured.

But the wine wasn't just a drink; it was a sedative. Jeff was playing a terrifying long game of chemical gaslighting. By actively encouraging her to be a day drunk, he was systemically eroding the very brilliant mind that had once managed his business and fiercely protected her own boundaries. While she slept off the wine, Jeff was reclaiming the house, the narrative, and the power.

The shock of the drug screen was the first crack in her wine-soaked reality. To see *Opiates* print out on a clinical report when she hadn't touched a pill was a moment of absolute, terrifying clarity. Sasha's instinct was to turn to her partner, the man she had nurtured, housed, and saved.

Jeff's reaction, a dismissive shrug, a casual muttering that the clinic had simply "screwed up the test line", was the ultimate tell. He didn't look shocked; he looked bored

The truth settled into her bones like ice: he had been secretly slipping something into her drinks. It was a chemical reinforcement to ensure her compliance and to keep her from noticing his own erratic movements. In the quiet confines of her home, the horrific trick of drugging her had become his ultimate weapon of control.

Inside the house, Jeff's performance reached a masterpiece level of duplicity. He remained the sad, pathetic mourner, leaning heavily on Sasha for every emotional and physical need. But the exact moment they stepped past the threshold of her front door, his mask flipped.

To the town and the neighbors, Jeff portrayed himself as the true Man of the House. He used his deep, assertive voice and lingering GQ presence to subtly frame Sasha as the unstable, drinking wife, positioning himself as the long-suffering, stabilizing force holding her together. He was systematically preempting her truth. He was making sure that if she ever tried to tell her story to the community, the world would already view her as a tragic, day-drunk addict who didn't know up from down.

The final stroke of his arrogant re-emergence was the show car. He used a massive chunk of his inheritance to buy a classic, high-performance Ferrari—a vehicle he couldn't even legally drive, a beautiful, useless object that served as a physical throne for his bleeding ego.

Sasha, exhausted by the burden of his dependency, welcomed the purchase. She was tired of carrying his weight. She wanted him to have confidence, to have something of his own; he was slowly becoming a burden to her.

She failed to realize that the sports car wasn't a sign of his recovery; it was a first flag of his violent revolt. He was building an entirely new life right in front of her eyes, funded by his mother's death and fueled by the opiates he was secretly feeding her.

The hostage situation had shifted once again. Sasha thought she was merely letting him out for recess, completely unaware that Jeff had already stolen the keys to the kingdom and was just waiting for her to pour another glass of red.

Her quaint sanctuary had become an elaborate stage, and the Ferrari in the garage was no longer just a hobby; it was Jeff's chariot of escape. While Sasha drifts through a purple haze of cabernet and television-show marathons, Jeff successfully weaponizes her desire for him to be better. He turned her into a gatekeeper who is too sedated to realize the gates had been kicked wide open.

Jeff's greatest trick has always been his ability to mirror Sasha's deepest desires. He knows she wanted the good guy, so he played the part of the devoted, dependent partner, soaking her in a comfortable pool of wine and domestic lethargy. By keeping her trapped in a cycle of day-drinking and uncharacteristic naps, he ensured she was too foggy to notice the shifting shadows in her own home. He isn't trapped with her; he is simply using her residence as a base of operations while he engineers his next move.

The Ferrari was the ultimate Trojan Horse. Jeff had masterfully articulated his need for *air* and *self-confidence*, and Sasha, exhausted by playing his warden, handed him the keys. She even provided the necessary legal cover, registering the car in her name so he could cruise the local streets in a vehicle that practically screamed for attention.

Jeff knew exactly what he was doing. He knew that a middle-aged man in a classic Ferrari rarely gets pulled over for a routine check; to the local police, he looked like a wealthy enthusiast, not a three-time DUI offender. He used the high-speed car to reclaim his mobility and his darkest secrets, leaving Sasha behind in her wine-soaked prison while he reclaimed his ladies' man persona on the open road.

The outside world, however, wasn't as sedated as Sasha. Her friends began to report disturbing sightings. Jeff was spotted in neighborhoods and at distant intersections that made no sense for a man just taking a casual cruise. He was venturing far beyond the designated blocks, rapidly reconnecting with the dark, drug-fueled parts of the county that Sasha thought they had escaped.

The most chilling revelation came from her own family. The unmistakable, acrid scent of crack smoke was clinging to his coat. When they brought it up, Sasha's astute mind performed the final, desperate act of self-preservation: total denial. She quickly dismissed the chatter, convincing herself that he had no connections left. She simply didn't want to know the truth because the truth meant the toxic power couple was back, and the demon was once again breathing the same air as her hanging plants.

Sasha had become a hostage to her own hope. She wanted the drug as far away from her home as she could fathom, but she is living with the very man who carries it in his fibers. By actively refusing to acknowledge the smell of the smoke or the mystery of his routes, she is effectively tying the knots of her own restraints.

Jeff has achieved the ultimate narcissistic goal: he possesses the financial security of her home, the legal protection of her car registration, and the total freedom to pursue his crack highs while she stays behind, guarding a sanctuary that has already been deeply breached. He was no longer her captive; she was the one maintaining the walls of a prison that only held her.

~~~

The feedback from her family acted like a bucket of ice water to her face. When they told her she seemed deeply drugged, early in the day, long before the first bottle of red was ever corked, the scattered pieces of the puzzle began to click. The positive opiate test wasn't a laboratory error; it was a physical manifestation of Jeff's need to keep her docile. He wasn't just soaking her in a pool of wine; he was chemically anchoring her to the couch so he could play the big man about town while she slept.
~~~

Her defense of him, that

"He has never been away from me."

felt like a lie even as she spoke it. The drives in the Ferrari were the only gaps in their twenty-four/seven proximity, and she now realized those gaps were wide enough for a demon to drive right through.

The smell of crack smoke on his coat was the final, acrid proof. While she was home, struggling with the confusion of a chemically altered mind, Jeff was out on the open asphalt, fueled by the hard and the thrill of the secret. The Ferrari wasn't about self-confidence; it was about logistics. It was a high-speed vehicle that allowed him to reach his dealer or his hook-ups and return home before Sasha's nap ended.

Sasha looked at the man who was now finally paying his own phone bill and paying her back. On the surface, it looked like progress. He had his own account, his own money, and a pristine veneer of independence. But Sasha knew Jeff's history too well. For a narcissist like Jeff, independence was just a clean word for privacy.

By paying his own bill, he had effectively shut her out of the only window she had into his digital life. He was good now, civil, contributing, but Sasha felt the underlying tension in his long game. She knew that a predator like Jeff never truly surrenders the wheel; he just lets the passenger think they are navigating.

They are now living in a house of mirrors. Sasha is pretending to be the content unsuspecting partner while secretly cataloging the smell of his clothes and the timing of his drives. Jeff is pretending to be the reformed grieving son while secretly dosing her and reclaiming his street connections.

Sasha's intuition, sharpened by years of psychological warfare, was screaming the truth: Jeff always had a final plan. He had successfully used her home to hide from the law, her clean name to rebuild his ego, and her body to satisfy his needs. Now that he has his inheritance and his Ferrari, he is preparing for the final act.

The GQ poster boy is fading. The years of vodka handles, hard chemical smoke he inhaled, and the heavy, sedentary lifestyle of closeted day-drinking have claimed his bowlegged grace. His alcohol belly has grown, and his skin, once soft and glowing with unearthed confidence, was beginning to sag and turn a hollow, distinct grey. Jeff was aging at double speed, his physical body finally reflecting the internal wreckage of his choices.

For a narcissist whose entire identity is built on being the ladies' man and the blue-eyed angel, this rapid physical decay was an absolute catastrophe. He knew he was losing his visual currency, which made his desperate need for psychological and chemical control even more urgent.

Sasha's growing lack of emotion was a terrifying vacuum that Jeff tried to violently fill with chemicals. He wasn't just pouring her extra wine anymore; he had escalated to systematic poisoning. By sourcing Vicodin from a local dealer and slipping it into her daily drinks, he was attempting to manufacture the desire that she no longer felt naturally. He wanted her to be physically dependent on the drugged, heavy feeling so that she could never leave him, even if her heart already had.

Jeff's behavior was now driven by pure animal survival. He knew that without Sasha's house, her clean record, her Honda, and her presence as his captive audience, he was absolutely nothing. His identity was a fragile house of cards that required her constant, validating gaze to stay upright. Without a punching bag to blame or a servant to manage his life, he would be forced to face the stark reality of his third DUI, his estranged family, and his dying business. He needed her to want him because her desire was the only mirror that convinced him he still existed. He wasn't just comfortable in her sanctuary; he was parasitically attached to it.

But the toxic power couple had finally reached its absolute expiration date. Sasha's brilliant mind didn't just resurface; it staged a quiet, ruthless coup. By performing her own controlled experiment, refusing his pours, dumping her drinks when he wasn't looking, and reclaiming her physical body through rigorous exercise, she shattered the chemical fog Jeff had spent months cultivating. The day-drunk, sedated version of Sasha was the only one he could control, and as her health returned, his power completely evaporated.

Jeff watched her physical transformation with a mixture of raw terror and boiling resentment. He saw her naps vanish, her eyes sharpen, and her body regain its natural strength. For a narcissist, a healthy, independent partner is an existential threat. He knew his GQ mask was rotting, his wine belly was visible, and his chemical gaslighting had failed. He was a man with several DUIs, a defunct business, and a childhood home he'd already been cut out of, living in an apartment where the owner now looked at him with cold, clinical indifference.

He knew she was onto him. He knew the opiate discovery was the smoking gun. In the silent hallways of her quaint home, he realized he wasn't the master of the house anymore; he was a squatter waiting for an eviction notice.

A man like Jeff does not simply pack a suitcase and leave quietly. To him, a quiet exit is a total, humiliating defeat. His narcissistic identity demanded that he be the one to deal the final, devastating blow—to leave a mark so deep that Sasha could never truly move on without the bleeding scar of his departure. He needed a meaningful, destructive exit from their situationship.

In his twisted logic, if he couldn't have her desire, he would settle for her absolute horror. If he couldn't have her obedience, he would secure her lifelong trauma. He was looking for a way to flip the script one last time; to take the cards she was holding and light the entire house on fire.

Jeff was currently assessing his remaining assets: the Ferrari, his only source of mobility and pride, though it was a legal ticking time bomb every time he turned the key; the remaining cash from his mother's death, which gave him the ability to disappear or cause a final wave of chaos; and his remaining access to the darker, criminal elements of the town, the people who didn't care about quaint homes or smart women.

Sasha had her smarts back, but she was trapped in an enclosed space with a man who felt he had absolutely nothing left to lose. Jeff was cornered, and a cornered narcissist always resorts to scorched-earth tactics. He was drafting a final chapter that she didn't see coming.

The silence in the house was no longer civil; it was the terrifying silence of a fuse burning all the way down to the powder.

CHAPTER 17: *Shattering the Pedestal*

As the early winter sun dipped below the horizon, casting long, bruised shadows across the floor, Sasha sat with a whiskey on the rocks. The sharp, clear clink of the ice against glass was the only sound besides the music, a rhythmic punctuation to her reclaiming of independence. She looked brilliant and undeniably sexy in her tight, strategically ripped jeans and cowboy boots, her sprawling posture entirely relaxed. She wasn't the good servant anymore; she was the sole owner of the future.

By playing "She's Waiting" by Eric Clapton, she wasn't just listening to a song; she was issuing a definitive manifesto. As the lyrics filled the room, the notes humming a stark commentary on the years of emotional abuse she had endured, she laughed openly. She was mocking the demon right to his face, letting the music tell him what her apathetic stare already had: she was done waiting for him to change, and now she was just waiting for him to be gone.

Across the room, Jeff was a tragic study in narcissistic collapse. The old GQ swagger was a distant memory. He sat on the opposing couch, physically and mentally squirming under the sheer weight of her confidence.

For years, he looked at Sasha and saw his own greatness reflected in her blind devotion. Now, he looked at her and saw a woman who found him utterly pathetic. In the harsh, unforgiving glow of the living room lamps, his wine belly and rapidly aged features were undeniable. He was a man out of time and out of tricks.

He was used to her yelling, her crying, or her drugged compliance. Her laughter and her whiskey-sipping calm were weapons he didn't know how to parry.

Jeff knew the meaningful grand exit he had been dreaming of was being preempted by her sheer indifference. He had tried to drug her, to isolate her, and to break her spirit, but there she stood, cowboy boots on, biting her bottom lip and smiling at her phone screen, completely untethered from his pathetic needs.

The December air signaled the end of the year and the final closing of their era. Sasha had no intention of sleeping in that bed tonight. She was finally awake, and Jeff was trapped in the nightmare of his own making. He realized that no amount of crack highs or Ferrari drives could fix the fact that he had lost his most valuable asset: Sasha's belief in him.

As the Clapton guitar solo wailed from the Alexa speaker, Sasha looked over the rim of her glass at the man who had once rung her bell. She didn't feel hate, and she didn't feel love. She felt absolutely nothing. And in that nothingness, Jeff knew he was truly, finally dead to her.

The December air outside was crisp and biting, but for Sasha, it felt like a baptism. As she strolled down the sidewalk, the rhythmic click of her cowboy boots on the concrete echoed the steady, healthy beat of her heart. She was finally breathing without the suffocating weight of his expectations or the chemical fog of his secret pours. In her mind, the quaint house behind her was just a building again, not a psychological battlefield.

But inside that sanctuary, the silence Sasha left behind was volatile.

Jeff sat in the living room, Eric Clapton's fading notes still hanging in the stagnant air like an indictment. For a man like Jeff, Sasha's confidence was more painful than a physical blow. By walking out the door with such casual ease, leaving him alone with his alcoholic belly, his ruined reputation, and no driver's license, she had stripped him of the only power he had left: his ability to affect her.

In the twisted, defensive logic of his narcissistic identity, her strength was an act of overt aggression. To him, her lack of fear was an insult that required a devastating response. He wasn't just squirming anymore; he was fermenting in his own malice.

Sasha's confidence was a shield, but it also made her blind to his capacity for malice. Jeff was still calculating. She assumed that since she was done with the game, the board was cleared. She didn't realize that for Jeff, the game only ended when he declared it was over, and he never, ever lost without taking something with him.

While she walked, enjoying the clarity of her own thoughts, the man in her living room was pacing her sanctuary, the home she had used to jail his ego, the kitchen where she had stopped taking his bait. He saw her pride etched in every corner, and he knew that to truly hurt her, he didn't need to lay a hand on her. He needed to incinerate the peace she had worked so hard to reclaim.

As Sasha reached the end of the block and turned to look back at the warm glow of her windows, a faint shiver that had nothing to do with the December cold ran down her spine. She had left a demon in her house, a man who felt like absolute nothingness without her control.

Jeff wasn't planning on being there when she got back. He was engineering his grand, powerful exit, the kind that would make him feel like the untouchable GQ poster boy he still believed he was. He was thinking about his mother's inheritance money, the red Ferrari, and the acrid smell of the hard. He was calculating exactly how to ensure that when Sasha stepped back through that front door, her peaceful sanctuary would be gone forever.

The silence of the December night was shattered by a roar that seemed to tear the very sky open.

Sasha stood at the edge of the gas station lot down the street, the vibration of the blast rattling through her teeth and knocking the breath from her lungs. For a split second, the world was a blinding, incandescent white, and then the orange-red bloom of the inferno took over.

Jeff had found his big and powerful exit. True to his narcissistic core, he couldn't allow Sasha to keep the sanctuary she had built. If he couldn't be the master of the house, there would be no house. He had used his old, dark ritual, the same arson tactics he'd practiced in his own property years before, to turn her haven into a bomb.

The gas smell he claimed to *love* wasn't just a high; it was the scent of impending destruction. By turning the burners just enough to bypass the ignition, he had turned the quaint rooms, the hanging plants, and the new furniture into a volatile container of death.

Sasha's intuition, sharpened by two years of grueling hyper-vigilance, had ultimately saved her life. That heavy tension she had felt in the air before she walked out wasn't just psychological; it was the physical weight of the gas-saturated atmosphere pushing against the door frames and walls. The brilliant woman she had fought so hard to become was now standing in the bright, mocking glow of her own ruin, her tight jeans and cowboy boots reflecting the fire's flickering, violent light.

Jeff was nowhere to be seen. Whether he had retreated into the darkness to watch the glow from the driver's seat of the Ferrari, or had stayed inside to ensure he was a permanent part of the tragedy, the result was exactly the same. He had effectively erased the physical evidence of their situationship, his rotting GQ facade, and the toxic power couple in one final, violent act of spite.

Sasha stood paralyzed, the sirens beginning to wail and echo in the winter distance. The demon had finally left her life, but he had taken her entire world with him. She was alive, her mind was beautifully clear, and the opiates were entirely out of her system—but as she watched the glowing embers of her sanctuary drift away into the black winter sky, she realized that Jeff's final plan wasn't just to leave; it was to ensure she had to start over from absolute zero.

Sasha stayed with her family after the embers finally died down and the police reports were filed. But as the winter weeks crept by, she realized that something was quietly, resiliently growing inside of her. Not an urge. Not a yearning.

A baby.

THE END

Author's Note

This novel is based on true events. While certain names, dates, locations, and structural timelines have been altered or dramatized to protect privacy and shape the narrative flow, the psychological warfare, the invisible knots of captivity, and the ultimate, scorched-earth destruction detailed in these pages are real.

Writing this book was not just an exercise in storytelling; it was a necessary reclamation of my own mind, my own voice, and my own history. For a long time, the shadows in the house were quiet, and the chemical fog was thick. Surviving a relationship with a high-conflict, malignant personality often means living in a constant state of hyper-vigilance, where your boundaries are eroded so slowly that you don't realize you are a hostage until the walls are already closing in.

To anyone who has ever stood in the ashes of their own life, looking at absolute zero because someone they loved decided to light their world on fire: you are not alone. The clarity you fight for is real. The return of your brilliant mind is a coup worth staging. Sanctuaries can be rebuilt, timber by timber. But the strength it takes to walk away into the crisp winter air, clear-headed and unbroken—that belongs entirely to you.

— Cheyenne Maryland Quinn

Stay Connected

Thank you so much for reading. If you want to be the first to know about future releases, exclusive content, and behind-the-scenes updates from Cheyenne Maryland Quinn, please join my community.

www.facebook.com/cheyennemarylandquinn

Or visit: www.cheyennemarylandquinn.com

www.ingramcontent.com/pod-product-compliance
Lightning Source LLC
LaVergne TN
LVHW100315210926
848480LV00003B/1129
* 9 7 9 8 2 3 4 1 2 2 6 0 5 *